William Alexander Baillie Hamilton

Mr. Montenello

Vol. II

William Alexander Baillie Hamilton

Mr. Montenello
Vol. II

ISBN/EAN: 9783337065089

Printed in Europe, USA, Canada, Australia, Japan

Cover: Foto ©Andreas Hilbeck / pixelio.de

More available books at **www.hansebooks.com**

MR MONTENELLO:

A ROMANCE OF THE CIVIL SERVICE.

BY

W. A. BAILLIE HAMILTON.

VOL. II.

WILLIAM BLACKWOOD AND SONS,
EDINBURGH AND LONDON.
MDCCCLXXXV.

CONTENTS.

MR MONTENELLO:

A ROMANCE OF THE CIVIL SERVICE.

CHAPTER XVIII.

" FLORENCE ! "

WE have already referred incidentally to the stable department of Gerard's establishment, and to the circumstance that, owing to the kindness of the Dowager Lady Narborough, he had been enabled to keep a horse in London at a much lower cost than he could otherwise have done. He was now, indeed, keeping two horses in her ladyship's stables, the second of which had only been in his possession a few weeks. One of his first thoughts on obtaining the appointment of private secretary, and consequently a certain increase of his official income, was that he might now be able to keep another horse;

and he had given all the powers of his
mind to the consideration of this important
question.   It was of course impossible for
a gentleman with the modest income of
£600 a year or thereabouts to think of
going into the open market and bidding
against others for high-priced hunters ; and
he knew that his only chance lay in picking
up something on speculation on an off-day
at Tattersall's—an uncertain and risky proceeding at the best of times,—or in hearing
of something from a friend that was likely,
for some reason or other, to be sold cheap.
In this matter he had been much assisted by
his chief, who, having an extensive acquaintance with horses and horse-owners generally,
and having gathered from him in the course
of conversation that he had a small sum at
his disposal for the purpose, had put him up
to the fact that in the draft of horses which
had been advertised as about to be sold
from the stables of that fine old sportsman
Mr Hill, of Whitelands, there were one or
two animals which it would be worth his
while to look after, but which were not
likely to attract much notice from the

general public. So it came about that, after
an anxious afternoon at Tattersall's, and
many misgivings and palpitations of heart
as he found himself responding to the
glances of the keen-eyed functionary in the
rostrum, Gerard emerged from the crowd
the possessor of a good-looking, iron-grey
mare, which had been knocked down to
him for thirty-seven guineas, and which,
had it not been for a slight string-halt,
would probably have fetched a good deal
more. Thanks, however, to the good offices
of his chief, he had learned that the mare,
in spite of this infirmity, had the reputation of being a safe fencer, and though
slow, in other respects by no means to be
despised.

So he had gone boldly in for a bid, fortified,
moreover, by the opinion of his friend Lady
Narborough's coachman, in whose company
he had inspected the mare on the previous
day, and who had been pleased to express
himself as on the whole in favour of the
proposed investment, and had cited his own
unbounded experience to the effect that a
string-halt, though unquestionably a blemish,

was not necessarily a bar to the usefulness
or trustworthiness of a horse.

It was with great pride of ownership
that Gerard contemplated his two steeds
as they stood side by side in Lady Narborough's stables. It is true that he was not
without certain misgivings as to the cost of
the venture in proportion to his limited
means; but he had gone carefully into
the matter on paper, and had satisfied
himself that with strict economy he was
now able to afford it. So he looked forward joyfully to an extension of his hunting
performances during the coming winter, and
felt as if he were equal to making a good
appearance anywhere.

The immediate attendant upon Gerard's
stud, whom we have previously mentioned as
a helper under Lady Narborough's coachman,
but who was now destined to enact the part
of stud-groom on his own account, was an
individual whose personal appearance would
certainly not have recommended him to a
casual observer as specially qualified for the
charge of horses. He was a long, lank, sallow-
faced man, of uncertain age, a melancholy

demeanour, and a general out-at-elbows look
that was not at all consistent with the generally accepted ideal of a young gentleman's
groom. When in his working clothes, and engaged in his stable avocations, he was a most
woe-begone and dilapidated object; and even
when at his best, and arrayed in somewhat
more respectable garments, his appearance
was suggestive of an undertaker's man very
much run to seed. At the same time, and with
all these external drawbacks, he was not without his good qualities. He was honest and
hardworking, and decidedly handy with
horses; and although at times stupid and
obstinate, had never been known to be altogether overcome by liquor. He was a man, in
fact, who, had it not been for his slovenly
appearance, might have had a much better
place than what he actually held. Gerard
knew very little, however, about his antecedents; for a helper's character is not usually
very closely gone into; and he had been
simply picked up for him by Lady Narborough's coachman on the recommendation
of a friend in the adjoining mews. But
Gerard had taken rather a fancy to him,

partly, it must be confessed, because there
was something about him that reminded him
of James Pigg, the renowned Mr Jorrock's
equally renowned huntsman ; and finding that
he really knew something about horses, he
had during the previous winter been in the
habit of taking him in the capacity of groom
in some of his hunting expeditions from
London. On such occasions he had, in spite
of his rough and ungainly exterior, acquitted
himself very creditably, and had proved
thoroughly reliable both in the matter of
money and sobriety. Gerard had therefore
come to the wise conclusion that he might do
much worse, and that his retainer's external
deficiencies were more than counterbalanced
by his intrinsic good qualities. So when the
second horse made its appearance, he resolved
to raise Martin's wages, and to endeavour to
smarten him up a little. This, however, was
by no means easy ; for although Mr Martin
had no objection whatever to having his
wages raised, it was almost a hopeless task to
attempt to instil into him any ideas of personal
neatness ; and the most that Gerard had
hitherto succeeded in accomplishing was to

give his stud-groom the appearance of a
fairly well-to-do scarecrow. But, smart or
not, he was the sole auxiliary upon whom
Gerard had to rely in his approaching expedition, and, as such, he determined to make
the best of him.

It was a fine morning then, in the first
week of December, that Gerard, who, by
making use of the colourable fiction which
we left him contemplating in our last chapter,
had escaped from the paternal roof and made
his way up to London the evening before,
was engaged in finishing his breakfast and
awaiting the appearance of Mr Martin. And
just as he had come to the end of his second
cup of tea, a ring at the door-bell, followed,
after a due interval, by a knock at the door
of his second-floor sitting-room, announced
the arrival of that faithful domestic.

"Oh, good morning, Martin, how are you ?"
exclaimed Gerard, as the door opened.
"Come in; I've just done breakfast. Well,
how are the horses ? You got my letter, of
course, and I suppose you're all ready for a
start ? By Jove," he thought to himself,
eyeing the unkempt-looking creature that

stood before him,—a threadbare black coat
buttoned up tight over his stable dress, a
ragged scarf hitched up under one ear, without a vestige of shirt-collar, and a tall, once-
black hat that an old clothesman might have
hesitated about picking out of a gutter,—
"he's a rum-looking fellow to have about
one. However, he understands his work,
that's one comfort, and I can't afford to be
too particular about appearances!"

"Oh, horses be well enough, thank'e sir,"
replied Martin, with a snatch at his lank hair.
"Mare feeds right enough now, and has put
on a bit of flesh; old horse uncommon fresh
too. Had 'em out this morning; both on 'em
fit to do a bit o' work now. Where might
you be going?" he added in a somewhat
searching tone; for he was of a stay-at-home
and unenterprising disposition, and preferred
the solid comforts of London, with an occasional day's outing that would bring him back
to the metropolis in the evening, to adventures
farther afield and the attractions of county
society.

"Oh, well," replied Gerard, "I was thinking of taking a run down into Wealdshire and

the Underdown country. I have some friends down there," he added, not without a certain feeling of guiltiness and an instinctive consciousness that Martin would soon find out his real object in going; "and I hear it's a nice sort of country, and the distances not very great, so that one might do pretty well there with a couple of horses for a fortnight or so."

"Ah, Underdown," returned Martin, with a peculiar sniff that was habitual with him when expressing a decided opinion. "Yes, they be good hounds, and a good enough country. Harriers, too, Littlebrook; go as fast as the fox-hounds on them hills. Old horse do well enough there; don't know about the mare, though."

"Why, what do you know about them?" asked Gerard in astonishment, having quite expected some opposition on Martin's part, and much surprised to find, not only that he did not disapprove of the undertaking, but that he was already acquainted with the county.

"Why, Lord bless you," replied Martin, " I lived there two year or more, down at Netherdean, old Mr Baldwin's, away by the sea there."

Gerard started as if he had been shot.
Netherdean ! Old Mr. Baldwin ! Could it
be possible that this ungainly creature had
actually been living in the same house, in the
same atmosphere, with his—his—alas! he
could not yet give a name to her—and had
perhaps been in her company every day! He
could hardly believe his ears, and stared at
Martin in a manner which caused that somewhat unimpressionable individual to wonder
what on earth was the matter.

" Why, Martin," he at length exclaimed,
recovering himself with an effort, and feeling
that it would not do to exhibit too great
emotion on the subject, "you never told me
you had been in the Underdown country.
You told me you had been with Mr. Jones
in Bedfordshire, and somewhere in Essex,
but you never said anything about Mr
Baldwin !"

" Ah, that were some time ago," responded
Martin ; " it were afore I went to Mr Jones,
like. Let's see ; it'll be a matter o' seven or
eight year ago now, and Mr Thompson o'
Scratton he were master o' the 'ounds then ;
nice gentleman he were, too ; but I hear he's

dead and gone now." And Martin heaved a sigh, and assumed an expression of melancholy that would have led the casual observer to suppose that, if not a near relation of the lamented Mr Thompson, he must have at any rate been one of his most intimate acquaintances.

"But about Mr Baldwin," continued Gerard, beginning to regard Martin with a new and increasing interest. "I know Mr Baldwin a little ; that is to say, I think I've met him. Let's see ; he's an old gentleman who wears spectacles, isn't he ? and he lives alone at Netherdean, didn't you say ? And there's a young lady, isn't there, a niece of his, who lives with him—Miss Graham, or some name like that ? "

"Ah, that'll be Miss Florence," replied Martin ; " nice young lady, too, she were, and learnin' to ride fust-rate. But Mr Baldwin, he didn't care much about horses,—fond o' beetles and butterflies, and such like. Where was you goin' to put up ? " he continued, evidently not particularly disposed to dwell upon the subject of Mr Baldwin and his domestic arrangements.

But Gerard could not answer for the moment. So he had found out her name! Florence—Florence—what a sweet name it was! and it seemed *like* her, too. Now he could think of her as his Florence, his darling; and she already seemed nearer to him. Oh, if only—— But he was recalled from his dreams by the reiterated inquiry of Mr Martin, this time propounded in somewhat peremptory tones, as to where he proposed to locate himself.

"Oh, well, I thought of going to Shaw-field, Martin," he said; "it seems pretty handy for the Underdown country, and I suppose there's fair accommodation there. I daresay you know it. Where do you suppose is the best place to put up?"

"Swan at Shawfield," returned Martin with decision; "ain't a better hotel in the county. Good stabling, too; good accommodation for man and beast. Mr Clarke, as lived with Sir Thomas Wharton, he kep' it when I was there; but in course I can't say whether he's there now."

"Oh, the Swan," observed Gerard; "why not the White Horse? I've been to a ball

there, and it seemed a good sort of place. Do
you suppose the Swan is any better ? "

" Well, you can go to the White Horse, in
course, if you like," replied Martin, with a
sniff; " but I know where I'd go myself.
Howsomever, that's for you to settle. What
time will you be starting, sir ? " he continued,
with another dash at his head by way of a
concession to appearances.

" Well, I'm not quite sure about that yet,"
returned Gerard, " but you'd better have the
horses ready to start in the morning ; and
if you look in here this evening about nine
o'clock, I'll let you know, and give you your
orders." And having dismissed his attendant,
Gerard prepared to indulge unreservedly in
the luxury of his own reflections.

" Well," he thought, as he proceeded to light
a pipe, and ensconce himself in a well-worn
arm-chair in front of the fire, " this is a most
extraordinary thing. Fancy old Martin having actually lived there, and my never knowing it till now. He must know all about her
too, and of course she will remember him. I
must get him to tell me something more
about her. She can't be any relation of the

old boy's, or she wouldn't have spoken of
him as Mr Baldwin. She must be his ward,
or some one he has adopted. And fancy my
having first heard her name from old Martin
too! I suppose I should have found it out
somehow or other down there, but it's nice
to know it beforehand. I mustn't talk to the
old beggar too much about her, though, or
he'll smell a rat; he's as sharp as a needle,
though he does look such a rum 'un. Anyhow, it's the most extraordinary thing that he
should have lived there." And so Gerard sat
and smoked, and thought himself into a pleasant
reverie, in which visions of Miss Graham, or
Florence, as he was now able to think of her,
mingled with pleasurable anticipations of
sport, and speculations as to how his horses
would get over the Underdown .country.
For although Gerard was most decidedly in
love, as he had for some time been obliged
to admit, he was not so far gone as to be
indifferent to the fascinating influences of
his favourite sport; and his spirits rose as
he thought of the prospect before him :—a
country of good repute, a couple of very fair
horses, and such an attraction, too, in the

background! Any lingering doubts, moreover, which he might have had as to the
wisdom of his proposed expedition, were dissi-
pated by this extraordinary coincidence about
Martin ; and he had very little difficulty in
persuading himself that there was a special
providence in it, and that he was only fulfill-
ing his destiny. Ah, Florence, Florence!
and he repeated the name over and over
till he got quite ashamed of himself, and,
jumping up and looking at his watch, found
that it was past eleven, and that he had a
good day's work before him. So, banishing
for the moment the thought of his lady-love,
he knocked the ashes out of his pipe, and
started off to put things straight at the
General Enquiry Office, and make other
necessary preparations for his departure.

CHAPTER XIX.

BEDDINGTON CROSS ROADS.

"Then I suppose, Peter, you ought to leave here about a quarter-past ten ?"

"Better say ten, sir. It's over five miles to Beddington village by the downs, and the cross roads are a good mile beyond."

"Oh, do let's start in good time, padre dear," broke in a third voice; "I don't care how early I get up, and it would be dreadful to be late. They say Mr Egerton is so punctual, he won't wait a moment for any one."

"Well, start when you like, my dear," replied the first speaker, a grave-looking elderly gentleman, who has already been introduced to our readers as Mr Baldwin of Netherdean; "as I haven't got to go, it's all the same to me. Well then, Peter, say ten; and if Miss Graham is not ready, it will be her own fault if she is late."

"Oh, I shall be ready enough, you may be sure," laughed the girl; "and Peter," she continued, "you'll be sure and put the new front on Kathleen, won't you? I want her to look very smart."

"Yes, miss, I'll see to it," replied the old coachman, with a smile; and, with a respectful salute to his master, he withdrew.

The following day was to witness a great event in Miss Graham's life; for she was to have her first day with the foxhounds, under the protection of old Peter, who had lived at Netherdean in the capacity of Mr Baldwin's coachman for many years. As we know, she had been in the habit of riding about with the harriers for some little time past; but her great ambition was to be allowed to participate in *the real thing*, and to be introduced to the glories of foxhunting. So, partly by coaxing and partly by teasing, she had at the beginning of the present hunting season succeeded in inducing Mr Baldwin, who, as we have already seen, stood to her *in loco parentis*, to promise that, under the strict charge of old Peter, she should ride out and "have a look at" the hounds some day when they met near Netherdean.

Beddington Cross Roads, as those who are familiar with the Underdown country will doubtless recollect, is at the junction of the hill country with the vale; and a run in that district is apt to present a very fair sample of the leading features of both. If a fox is found in one of the many sheltered deans that run up between the hills, or in one of the gorse coverts scattered about on their sunny slopes, he will very likely, in the first instance, take a line across the wide-stretching stubble or ploughed lands at the foot of the downs, thereby enabling his followers to make acquaintance with some nice little banks and ditches; but if there should happen to be no particularly inviting woodland to which he can make his point, he will in all probability turn his head to the hills again, and seek the friendly shelter of some wooded ravine, where he knows the chances will be very much in his favour. A meet at the cross roads, therefore, affords a favourable opportunity for seeing the country, and perhaps a nice little run, without the necessity for much hard riding; and is a very different thing from some of the fixtures in the regular vale country, where a heavy soil and stiff fences will often present a pretty severe test for both horse and rider.

For these reasons the meet at the cross roads had been selected by Mr Baldwin, subject to the advice of old Peter, as a suitable occasion for a young lady to make her *début* with the hounds. The old gentleman himself, it must be confessed, had not much to say on the subject; for although, as we have seen, equestrian exercise was not unknown to him, and he would occasionally accompany Miss Graham in her expeditions with the harriers, it was more in the light of a spectator than an active participator in the sport; and he was as a rule quite content to sit at his ease on a hill, while his equally unambitious steed quietly cropped the short grass around him, and survey the operations of the busy pack from a distance, till an opportunity should offer itself of rejoining his fair and more ad- venturous charge in a safe and easy manner. But fox-hunting was altogether beyond him ; and he had even resisted Miss Graham's entreaties to accompany her to the meet at the cross roads. "Peter will look after you much better than I can, my dear," he said; "and I'm too old and not enough of a sportsman to mix with a crowd of strangers at a covert-side. No, you will do much better without me." But sportsman or not, the old man had seen enough of the girl's riding to feel that she was not likely to come to much harm, and he had the most implicit confidence in the trusty Peter. So he let her go without much uneasiness, and prepared for a quiet morning with his books.

There are few things in life pleasanter than a leisurely ride to covert on a fine December morning, when you have not very far to go, and feel that you are in plenty of time. The fresh air, the elastic motion of the good horse under you, and the quiet landscape around, lit up into momentary brightness by the gleams of a winter sun, all combine to lend a peculiar charm to the occasion, and to bring about a feeling of contentment and general philanthropy. And apart from the pleasant anticipations of the coming day's sport, there is a certain indescribable beauty about a still winter's day in the country that is not to be

found at any other time of year. The luxuriant foliage of summer has long departed ; and
the glorious colouring of autumn, though still
lingering here and there, is rapidly giving
place to the soberer tints of winter. But even
a dull winter's day has a quiet loveliness of
its own that is often apt to appeal more
keenly to the senses than the more pronounced attractions of other seasons ; and as
the light breeze steals through the woodlands,
and the shrivelled leaves accept their ine-
vitable fate, and gently flutter down to their
last resting-place, it must be a somewhat unimpressionable mind that does not recognise
and appreciate the quiet if somewhat melancholy sweetness of the passing year.

But we have not come out to Beddington
Cross Roads this morning for the purpose
of moralising, and Gerard Courtenay, as he
wends his way along the road from Shawfield,
although by no means insensible to the beauties of nature, is, we fear, more engrossed by
anticipations of the day before him than by
the charms of the surrounding scenery. He
had arrived at Shawfield two days before,
horses, Martin, and all ; and having wisely

concluded that his own interests would be best
served by humouring that faithful domestic as
far as was consistent with the due preservation
of his authority, he had resolved in the first
place to examine the capabilities of the Swan,
keeping the more consequential White Horse
in reserve, in the event, which he considered
extremely probable, of the former being un-
suited to his requirements.   He found, however, that Mr Martin had not been far wrong
in his recommendation of the less pretentious
hostelry.   It was a quiet, old-fashioned, red-
brick house, rather in the outskirts of the
town, and standing back from the straggling
street, with a fine old elm-tree overshadowing
the horse-trough in front, while a corpulent
aquatic bird in a sort of Italian landscape
swung and creaked from a rusty iron bracket
over the door.   At the back was a roomy, old-
fashioned garden, well stocked with vegetables,
and with a row of bee-hives at the far end.
The internal accommodation was not elaborate,
but clean and comfortable as far as it went.
Gerard found that he could have a fair-sized
bedroom, and the use of a comfortable parlour,
adorned with some quaint old prints, an

ancient and decrepit piano, and a stuffed
cock-pheasant in a glass case, for a very moderate weekly charge ; while a couple of very
fair loose-boxes were available for his horses ;
and the landlord, who was no other than the
identical Mr Clarke spoken of by Martin, now
developed, together with his genial spouse,
into a rotundity that was decidedly calculated
to inspire confidence and suggest ideas of
good living and general comfort, undertook
to forage the noble animals at a moderate
advance on the market rates.   Altogether,
Gerard was very well satisfied with his quarters, and felt that he might easily have gone
farther and fared worse.

His first experiences, however, had not
been altogether encouraging. He had been
out the day before with the harriers, having
ascertained that they met at a spot on the
downs, which he calculated could not be very
far from Netherdean, and had fondly hoped
that he might meet Miss Graham.   In fact,
he had made so sure of her being there that
he had been grievously disappointed when on
arriving at the meet ‘he had seen no sign of
a habit among the little knot of soberly-

clad sportsmen, who eyed him inquiringly as
he rode up.   She might, however, not care to
come out early, he thought, and would very
likely join them in the afternoon ; and his
eyes were continually strained in the direction
of Netherdean, the whereabouts of which he
had ascertained in the course of conversation
from a jolly-looking old farmer, who, with the
usual well-intentioned compassion of a rustic
for a Londoner, which he had by some
process of reasoning divined Gerard to be,
had taken him under his protection, and
shown him the general "lay" of the country.
It was constantly on his lips to ask the old
gentleman whether he knew anything of
Miss Graham, and whether she was likely
to be out ; but he somehow shrank from
mentioning her name, feeling as if after all
he had come down on false pretences, and
had really no business there at all ; and as
no hint on his part would induce his friend
to volunteer a word about her, he was
compelled to stifle his anxiety as best he
could.   But the day wore on ; and though
his heart had once risen to his mouth by the
sudden appearance of a well-mounted female

equestrian over the ridge of a hill, a closer
inspection revealed a dashing-looking, dark-
haired lady of the Amazon type, and in
fact about as unlike Miss Graham as it was
possible to be. Then he began to wonder
whether she could be away, or ill; and he
had half a mind to ride boldly up to the
castle that contained his lady-love, and
satisfy his mind about her there and then.
So that day with the harriers was not particularly enjoyable for our friend; and, to
make matters worse, he was not quite
happy about the grey mare, which he had
ridden with hounds for the first time, and
which had got her head up in the air,
and behaved generally in a fractious and
uncomfortable manner, to say nothing of
having flatly refused at a small bank and
ditch, thereby very nearly discharging her
rider—who, as we have said, had no pretensions to be a finished horseman—over
her head. He consoled himself, however,
as best he could by the reflection, which
was indeed perfectly correct, that it was
probably his own bad handling of the mare
that had done the mischief, and resolved

to try her next time with a snaffle bridle. Having at length given up all hope of seeing Miss Graham, he left the field just as the afternoon was closing in and a drizzling rain beginning to fall, and retraced his steps somewhat dolefully to the Swan, where he passed a solitary and not very cheerful evening.

On the following morning, however, he awoke after a sound sleep, and felt his hopes reviving. It was a beautiful morning ; he was going to ride his old horse, with which he was perfectly at home, and whatever happened, he felt that he had at least a prospect of a day's sport. So he ate his breafast with much zest, and by the time the trusty Martin had got everything in readiness, he felt quite himself again, and eager for adventure.

" Cross roads be two mile furder by d' road. You go through d' ba'arway, and along by dey gates, and you'll save half a mile, sir." So saying, in reply to Gerard's inquiries, a smock-frocked shepherd obligingly pulls down the top bar of a sort of gateway, or "barway," as they are called in Wealdshire, and Gerard, hopping over the remaining obstacle, finds himself in a field-track leading through a line of gates in the direction of the undulating downs which stretch out on either side before him.

About half a mile further he emerges into a deep lane between high banks, with here and there an ancient yew-tree slanting across the road. Here he falls in with two black-coated sportsmen and one in pink, and at the next turn of the road he can see the caps of the huntsmen and whips bobbing up and down through the occasional gaps in the bank, while every now and then the crack of a whip, or an admonishing rate to a straggling hound, is borne back on the morning breeze.

And now the plot begins to thicken. A dog-cart drives past, with two muffled-up sportsmen, who exchange cheery greetings with the two in front of Gerard. Two more pinks appear round the corner of a copse skirting the lane ; and by the time the cavalcade have reached the little grassy knoll, crowned by a cluster of stunted Scotch firs, that indicates the position of Beddington

Cross Roads, the field numbers some eighteen
or twenty horsemen.

The huntsmen and whips dismount, and
look to their girths, while the hounds indulge
in a roll on the chalky greensward. Cigars
are lighted, mutual salutations and inquiries
pass from one to another, and the usual
"coffeehousing" preliminary to the business
of the day sets in vigorously. Gerard keeps
modestly in the background, conscious of
being the object of various curious glances
and muttered inquiries, but feeling at the
same time that whatever they may think of
him, they are not likely to find much fault
with the appearance of his mount. For the
well-shaped old horse looks fit and well, and
does credit to Mr Martin's grooming; and as
he steps gaily out, and bends his neck lightly
to the rein, he looks worth a good deal more
than he really is. Gerard, we need hardly
say, is got up in his best, in a well-fitting
black coat, and boots and breeches to which
not even the most fastidious could take exception. Both horse and rider, in fact, look neat
and business-like, and public opinion is on the
whole decidedly in their favour.

Meanwhile the field keeps increasing, and Gerard again looks out anxiously for the chestnut mare and her fair rider. Two ladies ride up, in one of whom he recognises his dashing-looking friend of the previous day. A third female figure is seen advancing in the distance, but of such ample proportions as require no second glance to convince him that it is not that of Miss Graham. And now the master has given the word for moving off, the hounds are eagerly clustering round the heels of the huntsman's horse, and Gerard begins to feel his heart sinking within him, when the click of a bridlegate behind him causes him to look round, and he sees an elderly and confidential-looking groom holding it open for a young lady on a chestnut. Can it be?— no—yes, it is! and for a moment everything seems to swim before Gerard's eyes. She passes close to him—so close that he can hear her speaking reprovingly to " Kathleen," that exemplary animal exhibiting some display of excitement on catching sight of the hounds,— but she does not notice him, and presses eagerly forward, closely attended by the trusty Peter, to join the crowd in front.

If Gerard had thought her rather nice-look-
ing before, how much more did he admire her
now, as his eye took in the graceful outlines
of her slight, lissome figure, set off by the
neatest of riding-habits, and swaying easily to
every motion of her horse. The keen morning
air and the excitement of the moment had
brought a lovely colour to her cheek, and a
gleam of sunshine shed a golden light over
her soft brown hair. It was a fair picture to
look upon, and more than one glance of admiration was cast upon her as she passed by.

Gerard felt a strange, indescribable exhilara-
tion taking possession of him. He had found
her again, his love, his darling, and he didn't
care what happened now. He had "thrown
his hat into the ring," and, come what might,
he would do his best to win her. So he felt
the old horse gently with his heel, and followed quietly in the wake of the hounds, content to bide his time till a fitting opportunity
should occur of recalling himself to Miss
Graham's recollection. It must be confessed
that he was not without an uncomfortable
pang of jealousy as he observed the marked
attention paid her by various members of the

field ; but he was partially consoled by ob-
serving that, with the exception of one or two
grey-whiskered fathers of the hunt, who evidently looked upon her with a sort of feeling
of proprietorship, she took very little notice
of her admirers, and was apparently entirely
engrossed by the all-important business of the
day.

And now the first covert has been reached,
a long triangular stretch of gorse, lying snugly
in a hollow of the downs; no road within a
quarter of a mile, and apparently the very
place of all others that a fox on the look-out
for comfortable quarters would choose for a
temporary resting-place. And so it is, and
many a fox has been viewed away from
Parson's Gorse, by which name it is known
to the many followers and friends of the
Underdown Hunt. But, as is so often the
case in hunting as well as in other matters,
it is necessary to look a little below the sur-
face, and beyond the immediate surroundings ;
and the eye of the practised sportsman, casting round for the points that a fox would be
likely to make for, is speedily arrested by the
now sober-tinted outline of Blackmore High

Wood, looming ominously in barely middle
distance, and in fact little more than three-
quarters of a mile away. If, as is highly probable, the fox at once makes up his mind that
he will have a better chance there than in any
of his other resorts among the wooded combes
and hollows of the downs, the utmost that
can be expected is a short gallop over a few
fields, with the probability of spending the
rest of the day in the deep and holding rides
of Blackmore Wood. But if, on the other
hand, he happen to be an animal of really
sporting tendencies, and feels equal to pitting
his own instinct and resources against those
of the clamorous and unreasoning pack of curs
that will persist in routing him out from his
snug retreat, it is quite likely that, despising
the friendly shelter of the neighbouring wood,
he will strike boldly off in the opposite direction, and make his point for a more distant
lair among the hills. Many a good run has
in this way been obtained from Parson's
Gorse; but it is at best a great lottery, and
many a keen sportsman, returning home after
an unsatisfactory day, has inwardly vowed
that he will never go near the place again.

Somehow or other, however, he always turns up again, in the hope that this time he really will be in for a good thing; and so the gorse keeps up its name, and continues to be generally popular.

On the present occasion we regret to say that, although the hounds had not been more than two or three minutes in the gorse before a slight whimper from old Rummager, which was speedily endorsed by the rest of the pack, denoted that the "little red rover" was at home, we should be unable, even if gifted with the pen of a Whyte Melville or a Surtees, to place before our readers an account of a brilliant run. For from the moment when he was viewed stealing along the ditch at the south-east corner of the gorse, it was evident to all the knowing ones that his tendencies were on the side of prudence rather than of daring, and that his point was Blackmore Wood. Many indeed were the exclamations of "Told you so!" "Always the same thing!" "Much better grub up the gorse and have done with it!" and so on, that reached Gerard's ears, and that to an uninitiated stranger who had viewed the fox away, and naturally assumed that it was all right, might have appeared somewhat unaccountable.

Gerard, it must be confessed, has not taken Blackmore Wood into his calculations, and in spite of the lamentations of the local sportsmen, is quite prepared to believe that he is in for a run. The fox has got away so quickly that he has not had time to come up with Miss Graham, who is now on the far side of the gorse, closely attended by one of the grey-whiskered old gentlemen already alluded to, and a stout, elaborately got-up young man, whom Gerard eyes with feelings of the most intense disgust. He has had time, however, to note that along the whole of the lower side of the gorse runs a wideish ditch, with a fair-sized bank beyond, and with no aids to crossing but a gateway about a hundred and fifty yards up on one side, and a sort of bridge or causeway about double that distance away on the other; and while he is wondering whether there is anything on the far side, the fox is viewed away. There is no time for further reflection; the hounds are already over the bank and into the adjoining field,

and the moment for decisive action has arrived.
A glance to the other side of the gorse shows
him Miss Graham and the old gentleman
topping the bank together; and even at this
moment of intense excitement his satisfaction
is unbounded at seeing the stout young man
scampering off vigorously for the gateway.
Now the huntsman shoots past him, and rides
straight at the bank and ditch, over which he
scrambles with a narrow escape from a fall,
demonstrating too plainly to any one who is
inclined to follow him that there is another
ditch beyond. But Gerard's blood is up, and
he knows what his horse can do; so disdaining
to follow some half-dozen of the field who are
making for the bridge, he gets him by the
head, and rides quietly at the place. The old
horse takes it "on and off" as steadily and
easily as possible; and in another moment
Gerard finds himself in the same field with the
hounds, and with the huntsman, Miss Graham,
and her elderly cavalier, as his only companions.
The majority of the field are congregated
towards the upper side of the gorse, in the
evident hope that the fox will break in that
direction, and take the only line that is pretty

certain to afford a run, and are consequently
for the moment "out of it."

"By Jove!" thinks Gerard to himself, who,
it must be confessed, was not used to getting
such a good start, "this *is* luck; I wonder if
I'll ever keep my place!" There he is, however, for the moment at any rate; so he scuttles
away up the rushy, undrained pasture in
which he now finds himself, and is soon in
the immediate rear of the huntsman. Miss
Graham and her gallant old companion are
still well to the front, and, in fact, perhaps
rather nearer the tail-hounds than a strict
master or huntsman would approve of. By
this time, too, the gate-and-bridge contingent
have come up, and form a highly respectable
ruck about a hundred yards behind; while in
the rear are the main body of the field, for the
most part a disappointed and objurgatory body
of sportsmen, loudly abusing Parson's Gorse
and everything connected with it.

The fence out of the field is a thin, quick-
set hedge stuck in the ground, which Miss
Graham and the old gentleman fly abreast,
closely followed by the huntsman and Gerard.
This lands them in another roomy pasture,

over which the hounds are now streaming in full cry. The grass is sound and firm; the pace is tremendous; and for the moment Gerard experiences that indescribable feeling of exultation and perfect happiness that few things in this world can so adequately supply as a good start with hounds. But alas! his happiness is short-lived. A few muttered expressions of disgust from the huntsman, alongside of whom he is now galloping at best pace, cause him to cast about for the reason of this discontent; and even now the outskirts of Blackmore High Wood are showing conspicuously on their left front. The fence now in front of them, too, is a black, impenetrable hedge of thorns, to all appearance hopeless of negotiation, and with evident signs of a deep lane beyond. The only visible outlet is a "barway" at the far corner, and to this they with one consent direct their horses' heads.

The hounds have apparently divided in the lane, about half of them diverging along it towards the wood, while the remainder have flashed across and are scattered over the field beyond. The huntsman forces his horse up the opposite bank and through a gap in the

hedge, closely followed by Gerard, who is determined to keep his place as long as possible.
" It's no use, sir," observed that functionary,
turning round to Gerard with a touch of his
cap ; " he's into the wood ; I know the way
of him well enough. But if you would turn
them hounds to me, sir, I'd be much obliged."
So, with a blast of his horn, he trots on in the
direction of the wood and parallel with the
lane, while Gerard, delighted at being appealed
to by such an important personage as the
huntsman himself, lets down the thong of his
whip, and getting the old horse by the head,
proceeds to enact the part of a whipper-in to
the very best of his ability. He is, however,
soon superseded by one of the regular officials,
who comes blundering into the field on a pulling, star-gazing brute that drags half the fence
down with him, and by this time the lane is
full of horsemen.

Gerard rides on with the huntsman, feeling
an access of importance from his temporary
association with that distinguished official.
The fence out of the field they are now in is
an up-bank, with a small ditch on the taking-
off side, and the ground rising beyond, so that

all a horse has to do is make a spring and
plant his feet well on the top, with nothing beyond to embarrass him. One of those places, in
fact, that from a distance look as if they required
some jumping, but are in reality extremely easy.
Gerard rides boldly at it, feeling that the eyes
of the sportsmen in the lane below are upon
him, and with his arm well over his face to protect him from the interlacing twigs overhead,
gets over very comfortably. The next field is
a rough, hilly enclosure, beyond which any
farther view is impossible; and an open gate
into the lane on the left appears the natural
and obvious exit. Gerard feels that for the
time being he has done his duty, and rejoins
the field with the pleasant consciousness that
he must have been noted as one of the only
three, besides the huntsman, who got away
with the hounds. The lane is now blocked
up with a noisy crowd, chattering and arguing
as to the line of the fox. Gerard has for the
moment forgotten all about Miss Graham, but
now looks about anxiously for the chestnut
mare. There are, however, no signs of her at
present, but he consoles himself by the reflection that, as they all came into the lane to-

gether at first, she must be somewhere on ahead.

A turn in the lane now reveals Blackmore High Wood in all its winter beauty, or, from another point of view, in all the hideousness of a hopelessly secure retreat for a fox that prefers discretion to valour. Deep, clayey sides intersect each other in every direction, and the grey and weather-beaten old oaks, of which it is principally composed, give shelter to the thickest and most impenetrable under-wood. Something must be done, however, and the huntsman gets together his now reunited pack, and dives into the uninviting recesses of the wood. He is followed by a section of the field, some actuated by the desire to be doing something, and others glad of the chance afforded by the sticky, holding rides of taking the fiery edge off their horses. The majority, however, remain outside, and discuss the chances of further sport, or explain to their friends how it was that they did not get away from the gorse with the hounds.

Gerard rides slowly on, feeling rather a stranger among the crowd. His thoughts have now entirely reverted to Miss Graham, and he wonders whether she has gone into the wood, or round the outside; and if so, whether he should go after her or hang about with the rest of the field. So he moves on by the side of the wood in an undecided sort of way, the old horse every now and then stopping and looking round, as if doubtful whether they are going in the right direction for sport. Gerard is just about to turn back and rejoin the field, when, coming to a sharp corner of the wood, his horse pricks up his ears, and he finds himself face to face with Miss Graham.

CHAPTER XX.

DEEPER AND DEEPER STILL.

SHE was bending forward rather disconsolately, with one hand resting on the chestnut's neck; and in spite of the attempts at encouragement of the cheery old gentleman by her side, her face bore marks of disappointment, which even its natural sweetness of expression could not conceal. "How very unlucky!" Gerard heard her say, as he approached; "and my first day too! However, it can't be helped, and that little gallop was *so* nice." At this moment Gerard appeared round the corner, and she instinctively drew herself up, though without appearing to notice him.

Gerard felt a little awkward. He had evidently interrupted a *tête-à-tête*, and the old gentleman was looking at him in a manner which suggested that on the whole his room would be preferable to his company. He felt, however, that he must not throw away such a chance; and instead of passing on, as was the evident desire both of Miss Graham and her companion, he advanced boldly towards them. Ladies are as a rule better hands at recognition than men. It at once flashed across Miss Graham that it was some one she had seen before, and as Gerard approached and took off his hat, with an attempt at a smile on his lips, and a heart beating violently beneath his corduroy waistcoat, she was not long in recognising her partner of the Shawfield ball.

"Oh! Mr Courtenay," she exclaimed, "is that you? I didn't know you at first in your hunting - clothes. Fancy seeing you down here! I had no idea you ever hunted in these parts."

Gerard had anticipated a question of this sort, and had prepared in his mind what he had intended to be a satisfactory explanation. But the sight of the face that had haunted him by day and night for the last month, and the sound of that gentle voice once more thrilling in his ears, had the effect of completely upsetting his diplomatic calculations; and he could only stammer out something about "Sydmonton — Underdown country — easy to get at from London"—and a few other utterly incoherent remarks.

"Oh, you are staying at Sydmonton, then?" inquired Miss Graham, catching at the name. "But that's a long way from here, isn't it? You must have had fifteen miles to ride, I should think. But I suppose you don't mind that, if you are fond of hunting?"

Gerard would have liked to reply that fifty miles more or less would have seemed as nothing to him, with the prospect of meeting Miss Graham at the end of it. He was, however, obliged to content himself with explaining, in a lame sort of a way, that he was not then staying at Sydmonton, and had only come from Shawfield, where he had come for a fortnight's hunting, having often heard of the Underdown hounds, and thinking he should like to see something of the country.

At any other time, Miss Graham might very probably have been struck by the evi-

dent confusion of Gerard's manner, and his
somewhat laboured explanation of his presence in the Underdown country. But her
thoughts being for the moment almost entirely occupied in various speculations as to
the prospect of further sport, his embarrassment passed unnoticed. In fact, although
Gerard was glad to escape the necessity for
entering into further particulars, he could
not help a slight feeling of disappointment,
however unreasonable, at being received by
Miss Graham with such an entire absence of
emotion. And as he looked at her fair face
and graceful figure, and thought what a
charming creature she was, and how she
ought to be admired, his heart rather sank
within him. There must surely be heaps of
fellows desperately in love with her; that
fat lout, for instance, who shirked the first
fence, but who was probably a great swell
in those parts, and very likely rolling in
money, what chance could he have against a
fellow like that? And no doubt there were
dozens of others; and yet, somehow or
other, she didn't seem to know many people
at the Shawfield ball, and seemed glad to have

him as a partner. And who was she? and
what was her position as regards old Baldwin? He must find this out somehow, and
by some means or other manage to get
to know her more intimately, though how
to set about it he was so far quite at a
loss. Possibly he might manage to make some
use of Martin in the matter, though this
would have to be very carefully done. Anyhow, Martin, if sounded, could probably tell
him something more about her, and he
would certainly try this.

All this time the huntsman and hounds had
been patiently working through the intricacies
of Blackmore High Wood, assisted or impeded
by a few of the field, who were anxious to
share in the almost hopeless task of inducing
the fox to break cover and betake himself
once more to the open. There was a cold,
intermittent scent, although a whimper every
now and then proclaimed that it was not
altogether lost. But matters were certainly
not looking lively, and a drizzling rain which
had begun to fall added to the general sense
of depression and discomfort.

Suddenly, however, the deep note of a

hound is heard in the middle of the wood,
and in a moment a burst of melody announces
that the game is not up yet. "They're running!" exclaims the old gentleman, turning
his horse sharp round. "Come along, Miss
Graham." And the words are hardly out of
his mouth before a brown shadow steals across
the ride a couple of hundred yards before
them. "Hold hard! There he goes!" he
continues, reining up sharp and holding up
his hand; "we may have a run yet." A
few moments of suspense, and the hounds
stream across the ride in full cry, followed
closely by the huntsman, who crashes through
the stiff underwood as if it were so much
paper. "Now come along, my dear;" and
away goes Miss Graham up the ride after her
ancient pilot, closely followed by Gerard. A
turn to the left brings them into a broader
ride, which runs out into a corner of the
wood, already occupied by a whip, who sits
motionless on his horse, prepared for immediate action in the event of the fox break-
ing on that side. And just as our friends are
within fifty yards of the cover, a piercing
view-halloo announces the much-desired event.

The wood is bordered by a rough, overgrown hedge, with a drop into the field beyond. Miss Graham and her conductor diverge to the left, and scramble down a sort of track. Gerard, however, burning to distinguish himself before his charmer, and tired of doing nothing, rams his horse at the fence in a somewhat careless manner, trusting to providence to get safely over. But the thick straggling growth has concealed the inequalities of the ground below, and though the old horse clears the hedge well enough, he lands on a greasy sloping bank, and catching his feet in a network of "growers," comes heavily on his head. Gerard described a complete somersault, but with the exception of a hat neatly flattened over his eyes, and a general plastering of mud, was none the worse. On scrambling up, however, and getting to his horse, he to his dismay perceived blood trickling freely from a cut on the off forefoot, evidently the result of an "over-reach" in his struggles to extricate himself.

"What a d——d fool I was!" thought Gerard, looking back at the nasty place he had come over. "Poor old boy!" he continued, patting the trembling animal and ex-

amining the injured foot. " It was my fault,
and not yours. It doesn't seem very much of a
cut ; but I can't go on riding him with his foot
bleeding like this. Now they'll have a run,
of course, and I'm out of it, and serve me quite
right. I must get out of this beastly place, and
find my way back to Shawfield." And gathering
up the reins, he was preparing to mount and
retrace his steps, when the tramp of horses
caught his ear, and looking up he perceived
Miss Graham and her companion riding slowly
towards him, and presenting no appearance of
participating in a run.

"Hallo !" exclaimed the old gentleman as
they drew near, " been down ? That's a nasty
place to come over ; you should have followed
us down the 'rack.'"

" Yes," replied Gerard, feeling rather foolish ;
"it was my own fault. I didn't look where I
was going, and my horse came right on his
head."

" I hope you're not hurt, Mr Courtenay ?"
inquired Miss Graham, with a semblance of
anxiety ; "you must have had a bad fall, I'm
afraid."

" Oh, I'm not a bit hurt, thanks," returned

Gerard, scarcely daring to look up in the sweet face that was bending down towards him with, as he endeavoured to persuade himself, a certain expression of interest. "My horse has cut his foot, but I don't think it is anything much, though it bleeds a good deal."

"Oh, dear, I'm so sorry," she exclaimed; "what will you do with him? Mr Percival," addressing her elderly friend, "do look at it; you are so clever about these things. By the way, Mr Courtenay, let me introduce you to Mr Percival. Mr Courtenay and I," she explained, with a slight blush and a hesitation that to Gerard seemed perfectly charming, "met at the Shawfield ball."

"Here, catch hold," said Mr Percival with a grunt, dismounting and throwing his reins to Gerard. "Now then," lifting up the injured foot, "let's have a look. Ah, I see; only a flesh cut; won't do him much harm; very likely be all right in a week. Lucky for you it's not a couple of inches higher; would have struck the tendons then, and laid him up for a month. You ride him home quietly, and he'll do well enough. You might

as well get the place washed out, though.
Where are you staying?"

Gerard explained, not without some embarrassment, that he was at that moment
domesticated at the Swan at Shawfield.

" Shawfield," observed Mr Percival; " well,
that's eight miles from here. Let's see; your
best way now would be over the downs, if you
knew the way, and past Netherdean. I daresay now," looking at Miss Graham, " Mr
Baldwin wouldn't mind the horse being
brought in for a minute, and Peter could
give the place a wash with some warm
water."

" Oh yes, of course," exclaimed Miss
Graham, eagerly. " Here is Peter," as that
functionary, who had never altogether lost
sight of his young mistress, now appeared
round the corner. " We can all go together,
—that's to say," addressing Mr Percival with
a tinge of melancholy in her voice, " if
you really think it's no use stopping any
longer."

" Well," replied Mr Percival, " you can
stop if you like, but you won't see much
more here, I expect. They will go on to

Raxton after this, I suppose, but that's five miles from here, and right away from Netherdean ; and if you've got to be home early "——

"Yes, I promised Mr Baldwin I wouldn't stop out late," she replied. " Perhaps I'd better go home."

" But the fox ?" inquired Gerard. "I thought he was viewed away—what happened to him ? Has he got back to the wood again ? "

"Got back !" grumbled Mr Percival; " I should think so—sneaked along the hedge-row there, and was back in that corner almost before the hounds were out of the wood. They'll do nothing with him now, but I suppose they'll go on after him for another half-hour or so before they give it up." ·

" By Jove, I'm in luck," thought Gerard. He had not missed a run, after all, and he was actually going to be taken to Nether-dean — to the place where *she* lived — the centre of the world to him, in fact. It all seemed like a dream, or some special inter-position of Providence, and he could only mutter out something about his thanks,— afraid of giving trouble, &c.

" Well, we had better be getting on,"
observed Mr Percival, who had now re-
mounted, " or your horse will be getting
stiff. I'll see you as far as Sellinge," addressing Miss Graham, " and then I must be going
home myself, as I have got a friend coming
down by the afternoon train ; but if you like
to take your friend on to Netherdean — I
daresay Peter will have a look at that foot
again."

So the three rode slowly off, followed at a
respectful distance by the trusty Peter, who
had not as yet delivered himself of an opinion
as to Gerard's fall, or as to the state of affairs
in general, but who had possibly none the
less taken in the bearings of the case and
formed his own conclusions on the subject.

" I am so sorry you have not had a run,"
observed Gerard to his fair companion, as
they emerged from the wood into a muddy
lane where there was not room for three to
ride abreast, and where, consequently, Mr
Percival, as the leader of the party, forged
ahead. " That wood seems an awful place,
and I suppose the next covert would be too
far for you on a wet day like this."

"Oh! it wouldn't be the least too far," she replied, "but I promised Mr Baldwin I would be back early to-day. You see it's my first day with the fox-hounds, and he thought I should be tired if I stopped out too long. But I shouldn't have been the least tired," she went on; "only he is so kind and thoughtful about me I couldn't bear not to do as he wishes. But I am so sorry about your fall, and your poor horse, as you could have gone on, of course, and they will probably have a run from Raxton."

Gerard would have been ready enough for a run from Raxton on any ordinary occasion, but in the present instance he could not help thinking that a ride home with Miss Graham the first day of meeting her was cheaply purchased by the loss of a possible run. However, it was necessary to say something about "his own fault,—better luck another time," and so on. But, somehow or other, the conversation flagged, and Gerard did not succeed in taking that advantage of the four miles road-riding between Blackmore High Wood and Netherdean, which, under the circumstances, might fairly have been expected.

Netherdean was an old-fashioned house of the type so common in that part of Weald-shire—something which, having begun as a farmhouse, had in the course of years ex-panded by gradual enlargements and addi-tions into a sort of manor-house or " place." It was built principally of red brick, which, by long exposure to the weather, had become mellowed down into a sort of French grey, here and there almost white, and only retain-ing its original colour in certain sheltered corners. There was nothing whatever of architectural beauty or design about it, and its component parts were incongruous to a de-gree. Some of the windows retained their old casement fittings, while others were of more modern and light-admitting fashion. On one side was an evidently modern wing, the red-brick colouring of which had not yet been sufficiently subdued to harmonise with the older parts of the building, while the stables and offices, which were attached to the house, had been rebuilt or enlarged with a mixture of flint and rough-cast. The whole was sur-mounted by a low, red-tiled roof, with a row of dormer windows peeping over the stone coping, and various irregularly-shaped chimney-stacks scattered about at intervals. The house stood back about a hundred yards from the road, from which it was separated by a low brick wall overhung with evergreens, and with a handsome iron gate in the centre, giving access to a circular carriage-drive, leading up to the front door. A modest, unpretentious-looking place altogether, but presenting the appearance of being thoroughly snug and comfortable.

Gerard, however, was not at this moment particularly disposed either to criticise or admire the points of Netherdean. He was now alone with Miss Graham, always excepting the presence in the background of the faithful Peter, Mr Percival having left them at a little village about a mile back. And as they approached the house, and he felt that he was actually at her home, and was about to be admitted as it were, for however brief a period, to her life and daily surroundings, he experienced an overpowering feeling of shyness and nervousness, and was in fact quite unequal to the occasion. Luckily for him, however, Miss Graham exhibited no such uneasiness.

She appeared, in fact, to look upon him rather
in the light of a chance wayfarer who stood
in need of assistance, and showed no signs of
being in the least anxious to receive him as a
visitor. She led the way up a side entrance
into the stable-yard, and was off her horse
before Gerard could dismount and assist her.
And here a slight awkwardness arose. Here
was Gerard, a comparative stranger, with a
slightly damaged horse, and to a certain extent
in a position to claim hospitality. And yet,
having got him there naturally enough, Miss
Graham seemed all of a sudden to be in
doubt as to what to do with him, and stood
for a moment irresolute.

She was relieved, however, by the interpo-
sition of Peter, who now came forward, and
touching his hat, intimated to Gerard his
readiness to examine the injured foot, while
a helper emerged from the stable and took
charge of her horse. "Then I will say good-
bye, Mr Courtenay," she said, with a slight
blush, "unless"—with a little hesitation—
"unless you would like to come into the
house while Peter looks after the horse."

It is needless to observe that Mr Courtenay

would have liked nothing better; but the invitation was not given in such a manner as to render its acceptance a matter of course, and he did not feel quite equal to taking advantage of it. So he stammered out his thanks, and his fears that he ought to be getting back to Shawfield, and so on, although all the time he would have given the world to leave his horse to Providence and Peter, and enter the charmed abode of his lady-love.

"Good-bye, then," she continued; "I am so glad to have met you again. Perhaps I may see you out hunting again when your horse gets well—or I daresay you have got another?" And with a sweet little smile, that went straight to Gerard's heart, she turned away and tripped into the house.

A few hours later, Gerard was sitting in his solitary room at the Swan, and ruminating over a pipe and the events of the day. He had accomplished his purpose so far, certainly. He had seen and conversed with Miss Graham, and had actually escorted her home. This was not bad for a first day's work. But, somehow, he was not altogether satisfied. He felt as if he had not made the most of his opportunity, and reproached himself for not having been a little more marked in his demeanour towards the fair object of his affections. And then, too, she seemed so utterly unconcerned; and although evidently pleased to see him, seemed to look upon him merely in the light of an ordinary acquaintance. Though, after all, how could he expect anything else? Well, he must hope for better luck next time; and she certainly did speak as if she would like to see him again. Oh, how lovely she looked as she said good-bye to him! And he tried hard to fancy that she had guessed his secret, and was not disposed to think the worse of him. So he mused and pondered, in a troubled and uncertain frame of mind, till he found himself overcome by sleep, and very nearly dropping into the fire, when he wisely concluded that it was time to go to bed.

CHAPTER XXI.

IN THE LIBRARY.

THE adventures of a young gentleman in love, although interesting to the last degree to himself, and possibly to the one other person most immediately concerned, are apt, after a time, to pall upon even his most intimate friends, and to become a positive nuisance to the world in general. We shall not, therefore, try the patience of our readers by following Gerard step by step through the various incidents of his stay at Shawfield. The day after his meeting with Miss Graham was peculiarly tedious. There was no hunting, and all he could do was to go and look at his horses in the stable, and wonder when the old horse's foot would be sufficiently recovered for him to go out again. A country town of the Shawfield type is at its best sufficiently dreary; but to Gerard, in his restless state of mind, its dreariness soon became almost insupportable.

He contemplated the possibility of going up to London for the day, and coming down again in the evening ; but found that it was too late for the morning express, and that he would simply have to pass the day in the train. He then began to consider whether he could with any appearance of reason or propriety ride over to Netherdean and call upon Miss Graham. But he could hardly summon up courage enough to venture on this ; and the idea of the mysterious Mr Baldwin in the background was somewhat repelling. A ride, however, would be better than doing nothing ; so, having hung about the town during the morning, he mounted the grey mare about two o'clock, and rode over the downs in the direction of Netherdean, feeling that, if he could not actually go and call at the house, it would be something to be near her, and indulging in a sort of vague hope that he might come across her either riding, walking, or otherwise disporting herself in the vicinity. But although he hovered about for some time, and went as near the house as he considered justifiable, he could see no sign of the form that was now dearer to him than anything in the world, and was compelled to return home disappointed. Still the ride itself did him good, and enabled him to get on better terms with his new purchase; and he found himself able to enjoy his mutton-chop dinner at the Swan, and even to take some mild interest in an ancient and dog's-eared novel which he found, among other literary curiosities, on a shelf in the corner of the room.

By the time, however, that Gerard had been at Shawfield ten days or thereabouts, the aspect of affairs had materially changed; and although he hardly dared to allow himself to hope that the course of his love was beginning to run smoothly, he certainly could not complain of being debarred from the society of the object of his affections. He had met her out with the harriers, and twice again with the fox-hounds, on the latter of which occasions he had enjoyed the rapturous felicity of a fairish run in her company over a nice, practicable country, the grey mare, with whom he had now arrived at a very comfortable understanding, having carried him to his entire satisfaction. More than this, he had actually met her in Shawfield, whither she had driven with Mr Baldwin one afternoon ; and had been allowed to take charge of her, and stand at her elbow in various shops while that estimable old gentleman was transacting business with his solicitor. And each time he saw her, he became more and more hopelessly in love.

And now he was to have a still better opportunity of enjoying her society than even the hunting-field could afford. He had been invited to dine with Mr Percival, the old gentleman who had acted as Miss Graham's escort and pilot the first day he had met her out. Both Mr Baldwin and Miss Graham were to be there; and there were rumours, which had received no positive contradiction, of a small dance afterwards. This seemed to Gerard to open up a prospect of an evening's unbounded happiness. He would be able to dance with her again—several times, perhaps —and if only he could manage to sit next her at dinner! He had received a verbal invitation from Mr Percival out hunting, who had at the same time casually informed him of whom he was going to meet; and during the day he had alluded to the subject in conversation with Miss Graham, and had expressed his delight at the prospect of another dance with her. For in those few days their acquaintance had certainly ripened into something almost approaching to intimacy; and Gerard would, to his surprise, find himself talking to her as if he had known her all his life. He could not help feeling that this was in a great measure due to the entire absence of restraint or embarrassment on her part; and could have wished, perhaps, that she did not talk to him in the same unconcerned manner as she appeared to talk to others. But there had been moments when a look or a word from her had set all his pulses throbbing, and had made him fancy that she guessed and sympathised with the secret of his heart. On that last day with the hounds, indeed, when they parted at the foot of the downs, just as a deeper glow was creeping up into the clear afternoon sky, and a slight feeling of frost began to pervade the air, she had given him a look and a gentle pressure of the hand that had sent him home in a state of almost delirious happiness, causing his estimable land-lady at the Swan to think what a pleasant and good-tempered young gentleman they had got for a lodger.

There is nothing new in the "old, old story." And yet, who is there of us who does not feel that his or her own particular story has something about it with which the experiences of others can only be flat and commonplace? Love's memories, as in other relations of life, are often made up of little things; and a word, a look, a pressure of the hand on some particular occasion, especially if during that sweet though maddening period when we begin tremblingly to hope that our love is returned, will remain engraven on the tablets of the mind and set the pulse throbbing long after other recollections are dead within us, and our hearts have become hardened and indifferent to what we once looked upon as the prospect of heaven upon earth.

A dance in the country is at any time a most welcome form of entertainment, and all the more so when it comes about in an impromptu and unexpected manner. Much

excitement had therefore been created in more
than one fair breast in the neighbourhood
by the report of the contemplated dance at
Crowhurst Park. The rumour, indeed, soon
developed into a certainty, various notes
having been received by those interested
apologising for the shortness of the invitation,
and explaining that the whole thing had only
been got up on the spur of the moment, principally at the instigation of a sailor nephew
of Mr Percival's, who was staying there on
a short leave of absence, and who would be
compelled to rejoin his ship in a few days.
It must be confessed that there were some
lamentations over the want of time in which
to prepare for the festivity, and the impossi-
bility of appearing, on such short notice, in
anything "fit to wear;" but somehow or other
everything seemed to come right by the evening of the dance, and at any rate nobody
would have thought of passing an unfavour-
able criticism on the general appearance of
the bevy of Wealdshire beauties who assembled
under Mr Percival's hospitable roof that December night.

There are few private houses whose resources

are such as to admit of a dinner and a dance
being given on the same night without the
former being in some way or other made to
give way to the latter. And although the
entertainment at Crowhurst was originally and
ostensibly a dinner-party, including among
the guests a proportion of the heavy fathers of
the countryside and their equally substantial
better halves, who as a rule would decidedly
object to their dinner being cut short, or their
symposium over the fire in any way inter-
fered with, it was wonderful with what good
humour they submitted to the arrangements
rendered necessary by the crowning event of
the evening.

It is not, however, necessary to the due
development of our story that we should
chronicle at length the progress of the Crowhurst Park dance. Let us rather content
ourselves with an extract, as it were, of the
night's proceedings, and take a glance at two
persons who, towards the close of the entertainment, and when one or two early-retiring
chaperones have already taken flight with
their charges, are "sitting out" a dance in a
remote corner of the library. To tell the

truth, indeed, they have been there during the last two dances; and yet they display no immediate intention of abandoning their position, which, shielded as it is by a heavy screen both from the fire and the rest of the room, offers advantages not to be despised by any two individuals who may be desirous of a little private conversation.

And yet, retired as is the situation, and comfortable the sofa on which the pair are seated, their demeanour does not on the whole suggest the idea of perfect happiness. The face of the lady bears an anxious, troubled expression, that contrasts somewhat sadly with the fair young brow and slight, girlish figure. Her companion is quiet and earnest, but also presents an expression of intense anxiety. Their actual conversation at the moment, however, would not strike the listener as of vital importance, or of a nature calculated to arouse feelings of anxiety or distress.

"How curious," she says in a half-interested, half-abstracted voice, "how curious that you should have got a man who had lived with us. Oh yes, I remember him perfectly. He was called John then, and I had almost forgotten what his other name was till you told me, but I remembered it as soon as you mentioned it."

"Yes, isn't it curious?" was the rejoinder. "I can't tell you how astonished I was when he told me that he had once lived at Netherdean. It seemed so strange to think that he must have seen and known you long before I did."

A blush was the only answer, accompanied by a downcast look, and a nervous manipulation of her fan. It was evident that the conversation was of a more interesting nature than might at first have been supposed.

He was getting nervous too. "Yes," he went on, "I told him one day that I thought of coming down to Shawfield to hunt, and I never was more astonished in my life than when he proceeded to tell me all about the place."

"But—but what made you think of coming to Shawfield?" she timidly and hesitatingly asked. "There's much better hunting in other places, isn't there?"

"Oh yes, of course, there are better countries," he replied. "But then, you know, the Underdown country is very good—don't you think so yourself? And it is so easy to get at from London, you know. In fact—in fact," he continued with some embarrassment, "I think it is a most delightful country, and I only wish I could stay a little longer."

"Why, you are not going away?" she said, raising her eyes for a moment to his, with a look that sent the blood coursing wildly through his veins; "you have only been here about a fortnight, have you?"

"Yes; I am afraid I shall have to go in a day or two," he replied. "You see I am not my own master, and I have got work in London. I wonder when I shall see you again?"

No answer. But the small, fair head was slightly averted, and the look of distress had returned. It was evident that matters were becoming interesting.

"It seems quite a long time since I first saw you," he continued, hardly daring to look at her, but playing nervously with the tassel of her fan, which she had half let fall, " and now I don't know when I shall see you again."

She seemed to endeavour to speak, but the words refused to come.

" Shall I tell you," he said, in a voice that seemed to him hoarse and unnatural ; " shall I tell you why I came to Shawfield ? " and, as he spoke, the hand which held the fan came, he knew not how, in contact with hers, and he felt that he could no longer restrain himself.

" Miss Graham—Florence," he murmured, " I can't bear it any longer. I must tell you how I love you. I have thought of nothing else ever since I first saw you, and this was the only way I could think of to see you again. Florence, Florence," he went on, wildly, having now got entire possession of her hand, though she still kept her face away from him, " won't you look at me, and tell me if I have any hope ? "

She turned her face slowly towards him ; but oh, what a sad, sorrowful look there was in those soft, gentle eyes! a look of distress and anguish that absolutely frightened Gerard, and made him drop the little hand he was still holding in his own. "O Florence!" he exclaimed, "what have I done?"

"Stop," she half whispered, wildly, "for Heaven's sake, stop. You must not talk to me like that. You don't know—— Oh, let me go, let me go!" And she rose hurriedly from her seat, and made a step forward, as if to leave him.

"Florence, Florence!" exclaimed Gerard, seizing her hand again, "you must not leave me like this. Tell me what it is, for God's sake, and forgive me if I have done anything wrong."

"Oh, no, no," she hurriedly replied, "but I can't tell you, and you cannot understand. Let me go, please, please," in a tone of passionate entreaty. And gently but firmly disengaging her hand from his grasp, she tore herself from him and disappeared from the room.

Gerard stood for a few moments dazed and stupefied. He felt as if he were in a dream, and that if he waited a little he would awake and it would all come right. He came out

from the corner behind the screen, and stood
before the fire, looking mechanically at the
clock on the mantelpiece, and wondering
what he should do next. A strain of music
came through the half-open door, and he
found himself listening attentively to catch
the air. It was the old " Journalisten " valse
—the one he had danced with her that first
night at Shawfield. Then he slowly came to
himself, and a feeling of unutterable misery
began to steal over him. He turned to the
sofa where they had been sitting, and, throwing himself upon it, buried his face in his
hands, and strove to collect his thoughts.
Then he remembered that others might be
coming in, and that it would not do for him
to be discovered there ; and he rose and
moved towards the door. There was something white on the floor, and he stooped
and picked it up. It was a little lace handkerchief she had dropped in her flight—yes,
there was the " F " embroidered in the corner,
and the faintest possible fragrance of some
delicate scent clinging to it, which he had
already begun to associate with her. He
kissed it passionately, and placed it in his

breast. "I'll keep this till I die," he muttered to himself, and slowly passed out of the room.

How Gerard got back to Shawfield that night he hardly knew. He had an indistinct vision of passing through the hall which separated the library from the ball-room, and finding himself in the portico outside, with the stars looking down coldly and pitilessly on his wretchedness. Then he remembered that he had left his coat behind, and returned to the cloak-room to look for it. On the way he met a chance acquaintance, who addressed some casual remark to him, which he must have answered rather wildly, as the speaker stared hard at his pale face, and then turned abruptly on his heel. Luckily, he found his coat at once, and again crept out into the open air. Carriages were beginning to take up, and hooded and cloaked damsels were being escorted out by their attendant cavaliers. Laughter and cheery good-nights were going on all round, and more than one glance of surprise and curiosity were directed at Gerard, as, looking neither to the right nor left, he made his way out at the door, and dis-

appeared in the darkness. As luck would
have it, he stumbled almost into the arms
of the flyman whom he had engaged from
Shawfield for the night, and who had by no
means calculated on getting his fare away
from the ball so early ; and in a few minutes
more he was jolting along the road to Shawfield.

Gerard sat back in a corner of the fly
in a sort of stupor. It seemed to him as
if his life had come suddenly to an end, and
as if he were in another state of existence.
The events of the evening seemed to have
passed away from him, and to have happened
long, long ago. And there he was, looking
out into the starlight, and able to think
what a beautiful night it was, and to wonder
whether the frost would stop hunting the
next day. His chief sensation was one of
intense weariness, and longing for rest. The
drive to Shawfield seemed, somehow, very
short, and he found himself standing at the
door of the Swan, and talking quite calmly
to the driver, while a sleepy boots was being
roused up to open the door. In a few

minutes more he was in his bedroom, and calmly preparing to go to bed. And, strangest of all, within two hours of his parting with Florence Graham, he was fast asleep.

CHAPTER XXII.

ANODYNES.

THERE is no truer saying than the old adage
that " Heaven tempers the wind to the shorn
lamb ; " and this is especially true in the case
of those troubles and disappointments which
come to us while life is still young. There
must be few who, when recalling some great,
and at the same time crushing sorrow, cannot
also, if they honestly examine themselves,
recall some little incident or episode, some
merciful dispensation, which has somewhat
softened the blow, and enabled them to bear
a burden that otherwise would have seemed
too great for human nature to endure. A
time may come, alas! when, the elasticity and
recuperative power of youth gone for ever,
and nothing left to look forward to but a
dark and hopeless vista of years, we begin to
realise that life is for us over, and that we
have been crushed down by a weight which

no power but the angel of death can remove. But while there is anything left of youth and hope, it must be indeed some very terrible and unusual sorrow that does not bear with it in its train some ray of mercy and some gleam of light that will suffice to preserve the soul from utter despair.

It was, perhaps, the best thing that could have happened to our disappointed suitor that next morning, when he was yet scarcely awake, and only just beginning to realise what had taken place, a letter from Lord Ravendale, marked "immediate," was brought to him in his bedroom, requesting his prompt return to London, provided — for his chief was always most considerate in these matters — that he had nothing special on hand that day, in which case another day's delay would not signify. The letter went on to state that in consequence of the sudden illness of the Secretary of State for the Aboriginal Department, Lord Ravendale had undertaken to superintend the preparation of an important measure to be brought before Parliament in the coming session, which would give him a fortnight or

three weeks' hard work, and would necessitate
the attendance of his private secretary, not
only for whatever assistance he might be able
to render in getting up details and particulars
connected with the forthcoming effort of legis-
lation, but also as a medium of communication
with other heads of departments on certain
points which were likely to require careful
consultation.

This summons, which under other circumstances might perhaps have been rather un-
welcome, was hailed by Gerard with a feeling of intense thankfulness. He had already
begun, in those waking moments, to feel a
sensation of despair and hopelessness stealing over him,—a longing to hide his head
somewhere, and be at rest,—while, at the
same time, he hardly dared think of what
he was to do next. And now it was all
settled for him, and he had simply to obey
orders. He roused himself, therefore, with a
great effort, and sending for Martin, informed
him that he himself was obliged to return to
London by the first train, and that he and
the horses might follow at their leisure. We
are bound to say that, under ordinary cir-

cumstances, Gerard might have felt some
diffidence in communicating such sudden and
peremptory orders to his faithful domestic,
who had made himself extremely comfortable at the Swan, and was by no means
inclined to approve of such an untimely
departure. But, for the moment, he was
regardless of everything but his own immediate concerns; and having packed his
things and eaten his breakfast with something of the feeling of a man in a dream,
he took leave of his genial host and hostess,
who expressed the most unfeigned regret at
his sudden departure, and just managed to
catch the 10.30 train to London.

On arriving at the office, Gerard was
warmly welcomed by his chief, and at once
set to work. He had a long day, and
scarcely a moment for indulging in his own
thoughts; nor was he even left alone in the
evening, which he could not help looking
forward to with dread; for Lord Ravendale
pressed him to come and dine with him in
Grosvenor Square, and by the time he got to bed
he was thoroughly tired out, and, to his great
surprise, found himself quite disposed for sleep.

It is true that on the following morning there was a reaction, and that as he opened his eyes in his accustomed lodgings, and the recollection of the last few days rushed back to his mind, a feeling of desolation and misery began to take possession of him, and the whole world seemed hopelessly dark and dreary. The reappearance, too, of Martin with the horses did not tend to raise his spirits, especially when that worthy announced, not without a feeling of secret satisfaction, as it seemed to Gerard, that the grey mare had got a cold, and didn't seem at all the thing that morning. But he was due at the office early; so, "pulling himself together" with a painful effort, he sallied forth, and was soon at work again.

A week passed in this manner, by the end of which, however, Gerard had had very little leisure for indulging in solitary reflection. The full weight of his sorrow had therefore been somewhat broken, and instead of brooding over and giving way to it, he had only had time to think of it at intervals. And although on these occasions he would feel

very crushed and sick at heart, the pain he
experienced had lost some of the sharpness
that it would otherwise have possessed, and
had subsided into a sort of dull and undefined
sensation of something wrong. Sometimes he
could hardly bring himself to believe that the
whole thing was not a dream, and that there
was such a person as Miss Graham in existence. And then he would have recourse to
the little relic of which he had possessed
himself, and the whole scene would come back
to him with a vividness that was only too
real. At these times he would go over all
that had passed between them on that event-
ful night, and would rack his brains with
thinking what could have been the meaning
of her strange behaviour. There seemed some
mystery about her—something which made
her different from any one else. And yet,
too, she had been so sweet and kind to him
with it all. He could not with truth tell himself that she had actually encouraged him, but
she seemed to take a pleasure in his company ;
and oh, how exquisitely happy those few days
with her had been ! What could it mean ?
Had he merely been too precipitate, and

frightened her by his sudden declaration ?
No ; there was something more than that,
and nothing could have been more decided or
more apparently hopeless than his rejection.
But give her up he would not, as long as
there remained the faintest ray of hope for
him to cling to ; and he passionately kissed
the little embroidered handkerchief, which he
now treasured as the most precious thing in
his possession.

What considerably added to Gerard's discomfort at this moment was the circumstance
of his having absolutely no one to confide
in or ask advice from. He had repaired to
Hatfield Street on the day after his arrival,
with the intention of unburdening himself
to George Morton, whom he now looked upon
as connected in a sort of way with the story
of his love. But he found to his disappointment that not only had his friend been absent
from his lodgings for the last fortnight, but
that he had left no address, and had intimated
that it was highly probable that he might not
return for some time. No cross-questioning
of the landlady could elicit any information on
the subject, except that, a day or two before,

a person dressed like a superior mechanic had
called with a note from Mr Morton requesting
her to give his letters to the bearer, but giving
no address.   There were a good many letters,
and she had handed them over accordingly.
The man either could not or would not answer
any of her questions as to Mr Morton's whereabouts, and she had not an idea as to their
destination.   In fact, she would not have
given them up, but that she knew Mr Morton's
writing so well, and knew, moreover, that he
would not be at all pleased if his injunctions
were not obeyed.   "For you see, sir," she concluded, "Mr Morton, he is rather a strange
gentleman, though we are all very fond of
him; and he has strange fancies about things
sometimes, and can't bear to be contradicted."

There was nothing for Gerard, therefore, but
to bear his sorrow in secret; and to do him
justice, he set to work to face it manfully, and
to make the best of any distractions that might
fall in his way.   As we have already observed,
his official work was the greatest possible
relief to him, and took him out of himself in a manner which at the time he was
hardly able to sufficiently appreciate.   A man,

moreover, who is the owner of two tolerable hunters, and is by nature a sportsman, must be very far gone in despair if he is quite unable to make any use of them; and when the first pressure of business connected with the preparation of the new Aborigines Consolidation Bill had subsided, Gerard found that, as usual, he had a day or two to spare every now and then, which—with some little effort at first—he devoted pretty regularly to hunting from London.

Somehow or other, therefore, the time slipped away, till Gerard found to his astonishment one morning that it was six weeks since that memorable night at Crowhurst Park. He had passed his Christmas quietly and sadly enough in London, having been glad of the excuse afforded by the pressure of his official work for not going down to his own people. And although he could not yet bring himself to think calmly of what had passed, and was still inclined to take a gloomy view of life in general, it had unquestionably been to a certain extent softened down. On hunting days, indeed, he would feel almost himself, and for a time forget his troubles altogether; and he was now looking forward with a sort of melancholy pleasure to an approaching visit to the Mount-Eastons at Bellmoor, one of Lord St Ives' numerous places, which was for the time occupied by his eldest son and his family, and where there was to be a small party to finish up the shooting. It would be a relief, he thought, to see and have a talk to Lady Mount-Easton; and perhaps he might venture to confide his love affairs to her, and come in for a little sympathy and good advice.

And so it fell out that late one afternoon towards the end of January, Gerard found himself landed on the platform at a junction on the North-Western Railway, somewhere on the borders of Westmoreland and York-shire, and waiting for a cross-country train that was to take him on to his destination. It was a chilly, wild evening, and after some seven hours' confinement in a railway carriage, and with the prospect of another hour and a half before him, he was glad of the oppor-tunity of stretching his legs; and having superintended the changing of his luggage, and ascertained that his train would not start for another half-hour, owing to the lateness of the south express for which it was timed to wait, he set to work to walk briskly up and down the platform.

There is a good deal more poetry and romance about railway travelling than is generally supposed. We will not go so far as to say that there is anything particularly suggestive of either in the general appearance and surroundings of a station on the underground railway, a London terminus on a foggy winter morning, or an average railway refreshment-room. These, however, are mere details; and if the idea of poetry may be associated with that of power, the stupendous force of steam may surely be considered as affording a fit subject for the poet as well as for the scientific man. Nor is the poetry of steam locomotion to be confined to the mere vastness of the invention; for, if only we take the trouble to look for them, it is difficult to avoid being struck by the many points of interest which present themselves to the eye in the course of almost any railway journey of a few hours' duration. It is but rarely that a railway scene has been selected as a subject for the artist; and yet in these days, when almost every possible incident of every-day life has been represented in every conceivable form, until it would seem impossible to find a subject that had not already been worn threadbare, it seems strange that such a field as is offered by the many and various incidents connected with railway travelling should not have been more utilised. It may perhaps be thought almost profane to suggest that the picturesqueness of a landscape could be improved by such a commonplace object as a line of railway ; but if there is anything in the force of contrast, as we are generally taught to believe, it would be difficult to find anything more effective than the combination, under certain conditions, of the triumphs of human skill with the quiet majesty of nature.

It is not our business, however, to write a treatise on railways in connection with art, either pictorial or poetical ; and it will be sufficient for our purpose to observe that as Gerard waited for his train on this particular occasion, he could not help being struck by the picturesque appearance which the approach of evening had begun to impart to

the surroundings of what is recorded pro-
saically enough in Bradshaw as Long Heaton
Junction. It had been a wild, stormy day,
and there was still a good deal of wind; but
the rain had passed off, and the moon was
rising in a clear sky, only occasionally ob-
scured by a rapidly drifting cloud. Gerard
went out to the extreme end of the platform
and looked about him. The station was
situated just at the edge of a wild moorland district, which stretched away on one
side towards the now dim and indistinct
hills in the far distance, while on the other
the mist was beginning to rise from the
low-lying fields in the valley up which the
line had wound for some miles. The station
buildings, which the approach of night had
relieved of their natural stiffness and an-
gularity, formed a dark, shadowy mass in
the foreground, and the converging lines of
rails, now glistening in the moonlight,
stretched away into the distance until lost
sight of round a curve where a tall signal
post stood up sharply against the sky, with
a red light twinkling from its summit. Other
lights, white, red, and green, began to spring

up all round in a mysterious manner, and to
reflect themselves in a dark reservoir con-
structed for the supply of water to the engines, which by daylight might have looked
artificial and commonplace enough, but which,
in the shadows of night, and out there on the
moorland, might with a very slight stretch of
imagination have passed for a natural tarn.
The bustle of the station had subsided with
the departure of the last train; and scarcely
a sound was to be heard but the ceaseless
music of the wind among the telegraph wires,
and a mysterious rumbling from the hollows
of the distant hills, where some heavy goods
train was slowly labouring up a steep incline.

Gerard stood for a few moments enjoying
the fresh evening air, and thinking how de-
licious it would be if by any possibility he
were going to meet Miss Graham at Bellmoor;
and then, beginning to feel rather chilly, retraced his steps along the platform. The train
by which he was to continue his journey
was drawn up in a siding, and all ready to
start. The engine was already attached, and
there was a great bubbling of water going on

in the tender, with occasional puffs of steam, and other mysterious noises indicative of a desire to be off. The driver and fireman were leaning over the side-rail together, smoking and staring out into the darkness, occasionally exchanging a monosyllabic remark, but otherwise to all appearance half asleep. Gerard had completed two or three turns of the platform without bestowing more than a casual glance upon the engine; but as he passed by for the fourth time, he observed that one of the men appeared to be looking intently at him. He thought nothing of this, however, and passed on; but as he turned at the other end of the deserted platform, he noticed that the man had got off the engine, and was advancing slowly towards him. They passed each other within a couple of yards, and somehow or other there seemed to be something familiar to Gerard in the man's appearance. He was tall and broad-shouldered, with a slight stoop; but as he had a fur cap drawn over his eyes, and the lower part of his face was concealed by the turned-up collar of a heavy pilot-coat, there was scarcely enough of his features visible in the dim light for purposes of identification. They passed and re-passed twice; but at the third meeting the stranger seemed to have satisfied his mind on the subject, for instead of passing Gerard again, he stopped short in front of him, and pushing his cap back from his forehead, emitted a grunt of recognition.

Gerard started back in amazement.   It was George Morton!

CHAPTER XXIII.

MOSSHOPE FELL.

WHEN two friends meet suddenly and un-expectedly, their greetings to each other for the first few moments are apt to be somewhat incoherent. Gerard was so com-pletely taken aback by coming across Morton in this most unforeseen manner that he could only stare at him, and make use of one or two broken expressions of astonishment. "George! By Jove! is it possible?" he exclaimed at length. "Why, what the devil are you doing here?"

"Doing?" replied Morton, who was more collected; "well, if you particularly want to know, I'm engine-driving — going to work this train to Starlington as soon as the South express comes in."

"But, my dear fellow," returned Gerard, in the greatest amazement, "what on earth made you take to this sort of thing? I have been wondering what the deuce had become of you—thought you must have gone back to South America or somewhere ; but this beats everything."

"Well, Jerry, old boy," replied the other, "there are some things that take a deal of telling, and this is hardly the time and place for a long story. Perhaps I may tell you some day, but in the meantime, you understand, I'm here on the quiet, and I don't particularly care about my whereabouts being known. I had some doubts about speaking to you, but, somehow, I couldn't help it."

"George, old man," replied Gerard, with warmth, "you know you can trust me, and I'll keep it dark, no fear. But only fancy you being an engine-driver ! What on earth put that into your head ? "

"Well, my dear fellow, after all there's nothing so very remarkable in it. You see, I was brought up for this business once, and why shouldn't I take to it again for a bit ? But never mind me, Jerry, just now, and tell me about yourself. How are you getting on, and how's the young woman down at—— Ah, let's see, I've forgotten the name of the place now."

"George, old man," replied Gerard hurriedly, " I'm so glad I've met you, for it's the very thing I wanted to talk to you about." And he proceeded to impart to his friend as briefly as possible what had happened, and how his expedition to Shawfield had ended in sorrow and disappointment. " But, George, old fellow," he went on, " I don't mean to give her up, I can tell you ; though sometimes I feel very hopeless and miserable. I'm awfully glad I've met you, as I was longing to have a talk to some one about it, and there's no one else I should much care to tell it to."

" Well, Jerry, old boy," returned Morton, with a friendly pressure of his arm, "you know you can trust me, and I'm glad you should like to tell me all about the business. But cheer up, old fellow, and perhaps it will all come right some day. That South train's very late to-night; I'll just go into the office and see where she is."

"I say, George," exclaimed Gerard, " I'm going by this train, you know, as far as Bellmoor. Can't I come with you on the engine ? it would be great fun."

" Well, I don't know about that," replied

Morton, doubtfully; "it's against all the rules, you know, and some fellow might make himself nasty about it. However, I'll see the stationmaster, who's a good sort of fellow, and knows I wouldn't be likely to play the fool, and perhaps we may manage it on the quiet. You wait here till I come back," and he went off to the stationmaster's office.

"Well," he said, on rejoining Gerard, "I've squared it, though he doesn't half like it; but the train won't be full, and being dark, let's hope no one will notice it. Look here; show me where your things are, and I'll say a word to the guard, so that he will know what to do with them."

"By Jove, what a lark!" exclaimed Gerard, in delight. "My small things are in one of these carriages,—oh, here they are,—and my luggage is all right in the van, for I saw it put in."

"All right," said Morton. "Now then, the South train is only about three miles off, and will be here directly. As soon as she comes in sight round that curve, you just slip quietly down by the end of the platform there, and come round on the off side of my engine. I'll

give you the word to get up just before we
start, and then no one will see you. Oh!
here's the guard; I'll just say a word to him,
and if you like to give him half-a-crown afterwards, it will make it all right. I must go
and see after the engine now."

Gerard obeyed his instructions implicitly.
In a minute or two the whistle of the South
express was heard, still some distance away
on the moorland. The station began to wake
up; porters appeared from various corners;
the few passengers who were going by the
branch train, and who had not already taken
their seats, emerged from the waiting-room,
and began to bustle about as if they had not
a moment to spare. Gerard walked to the
end of the platform, and as the head-lights of
the approaching train came into view round
the curve, stepped down on to the rails, and
slipping round to the far side of the engine of
the waiting train, took up his position under
the friendly shadow of an empty goods truck.
The South train came gliding on, the huge
express engine seeming to tower above him as
he stood on the ground, and drew up at the
platform. There was a ringing of bells, a

shouting of porters, and rumbling of luggage-trucks; and then a momentary lull, a cry of "Any more going on?" a sharp whistle, and the train was off again.

The whole remaining interest of Long Heaton Junction was now concentrated on Gerard's train, already kept waiting some twenty minutes over its time. As Gerard stood in his concealment, he could hear the stationmaster and guard adjuring the passengers who had changed from the South train to make haste, as the Starlington train was very late, and there was not a moment to spare. He kept his eyes fixed on the engine, in expectation of Morton's signal; and in a another minute a figure came to the side, and .beckoned to him with a low whistle. Gerard hurried up, and, aided by the friendly hand of the fireman, climbed up the ladder-like iron steps of the engine, and found himself on the footplate. Morton was leaning over the other side, looking out intently for the signal to start. He looked round, and nodded to Gerard; but in another moment the guard's whistle was heard, and, with an acknowledging wave of the hand, he seized the regulator, gave a sharp jerk to the steam whistle, and they were off.

The sensation of being on a railway engine was quite new to our friend Gerard, and he had some doubts as to where he ought to stand, and how to behave generally. Morton was peering out fixedly into the half darkness, and apparently completely absorbed in his duties ; but his friend the fireman now came to his assistance, and indicated a corner where he would be out of the way, while he himself opened the furnace door and began to stoke vigorously, the flood of light that burst forth producing a most picturesque and Rembrandt-like effect on the shining machinery, the dark figures of the driver and fireman, and the black mass of the train behind. There was something, too, about the motion of the now rapidly-gliding engine that was peculiarly exhilarating ; and as they rushed through the fresh night air Gerard felt his spirits rising, and began to think that life on an engine must be rather a pleasant thing.

A rattle and jolting of points, a flash of red and white signals, and they were past the junction, and gliding smoothly along the

diverging line across the moor. This point
of danger past, Morton relaxed his vigilance
for a moment, and beckoned to Gerard to
cross over to his side of the engine. "All
right now, old fellow," he said; "you stand
behind me, and then you'll be out of the
way. Glad to see you've got your ulster on;
you'll find it cold before you've done with
it."

"George, old boy, I think it's capital fun,"
replied Gerard. "I must say, you're quite
the engine-driver, and no mistake. Why,
one would think you had been at it all your
life."

"Ah," rejoined Morton, with a sad smile,
"well, I must say that if you want to get
taken out of yourself, I know nothing better.
Won't do to think of anything else when
you're running through a station at forty
miles an hour, and have got to look out for
signals. There's one now," he continued,
as a twinkling white light appeared some
distance in front of them; "that's the Cano-
bie distance signal, and we're sometimes
stopped there; but it's all right to-night, so
we shall run right through."

"This is a quick train, isn't it?" inquired Gerard; "we seem to be going no end of a pace now."

"Yes, we run hard to Corby Bridge, twenty-three miles, without stopping; and then there are only two stoppages between that and Bell-moor, where you get off."

"I say, George," suddenly exclaimed Gerard, in alarm, "where's the other fellow?—he's gone: why, he must have tumbled off!"

"Oh, he's right enough," replied Morton, smiling, "he's only gone forward to see to the head-light, or something. Here he is again," as a figure suddenly appeared on the other side of the engine, and joined them on the footplate. "Rum old fellow," he muttered to Gerard; "Ezekiel is his name—Ezekiel Jones; they run a good deal on Scripture names down here. Don't talk much, but a good old chap, and been on this road ever so long."

So they rushed on through the darkness, Morton occasionally exchanging a few words with Gerard, but all the time never relaxing his look-out ahead, except now and then to alter the position of the regulator, or turn

certain other mysterious - looking handles.
The prophetically-named fireman, a wooden-
faced, impassive-looking individual, who might
have been any age between forty and sixty,
had now relighted his pipe by the process of
inserting a long iron rod into the furnace
until it became red-hot, and leaning against
the brake-handle with his arms folded, kept
the same watch on his own side. They flew
past station after station, sometimes with a
touch of the steam-whistle by the driver, at
others with no sign but the wave of a lamp
from a solitary stationmaster or porter on a
lonely platform. At length a twinkling of
many lights began to manifest itself some
distance ahead. Morton suddenly pushed
back his regulator as far as it would go, and
began to look anxiously round the corner of
the weather-board, while the fireman applied
himself diligently to the wheel of the brake,
and the speed of the train began to per-
ceptibly slacken. Two or three short, sharp
whistles from the engine were responded to
by a grinding and scraping from the brakes
on the carriages behind, and in a few moments
the train was almost at a standstill.

"Signals against us," muttered Morton to Gerard, "something shunting at the station, probably. Ah! it's all right now;" and with a sharp touch of the whistle, and a whirling round of the brake, they shot on again, and pulled up at the platform of Corby Bridge.

The moment the train stopped, Morton was off the engine, with a long-spouted oil-can in his hand, and Gerard, looking over the side, could see him poking about among the machinery, inserting the spout here and there, and examining certain confidential localities with the greatest care. Having thus made a circuit of the engine, he reascended on the off-side, and resumed his conversation with Gerard. "We shall be here five minutes or so," he said; "we wait for a short train from Tarnforth, and she's not in yet. Hallo! there's the up-train coming in. There's a queer old fellow drives it, I should like you to see him; been on this road over thirty years; he's a scriptural cove too, Elijah Wilson they call him. Zeke," turning to the fireman, "those are Elijah's lights, eh?"

The fireman, thus apostrophised, looked over the side of the engine at the lights of an

advancing train, and with a nod of his head
and an elongation of a mouth the dimensions
of which had certainly not been contracted by
nature, intimated his opinion that the lights
in question were no other than Elijah's.   On
came the train, and drew up at the opposite
platform, the two engines being almost abreast.
The driver of the newly-arrived train swung
himself off, and proceeded to go through the
same evolutions with an oil-can that Morton
had already performed on his own account;
and having seen that all was right, and regained his foot-plate, looked across and greeted
Morton and his fireman.

"Good   evening,   Mr   Wilson," observed
Morton, in return to the other's salutation;
"how's the bank to-night?"

"Ah, lad, it's just fine," was the answer;
"ye'll no' need the pilot up Mosshope Bank
the night.   But ye're late; ye should be atop
o' Summit by this time."

The speaker was a tall, powerful-looking,
elderly man, with grizzled hair and beard, a
weather-beaten face, and a keen piercing eye,
that seemed always looking into space.   His
upper lip was shaved, showing deeply indented

lines about a mouth the expression of which denoted energy and decision. The sort of face, in fact, that one would be glad to see on one's side in a life-and-death struggle, or on any occasion where courage and presence of mind are called into play. And where is this more likely to be the case than in the daily life of an engine-driver—a man who carries in his hand not only his own life, but the lives of thousands of others? Yet he is one of a class of men little known, still less understood, and rarely given a thought to, except perhaps when a column or two of the daily papers are taken up with the report of some ghastly railway accident, and we read how a driver or fireman, after doing everything in his power to avert a collision or save a train that had gone off the rails, had been found buried in the ruins of his engine, to which he had stuck to the last with a dogged and self-sacrificing obstinacy, knowing all the time that he was rushing into the jaws of death.

" Yes," returned Morton ; " had to wait half an hour at Long Heaton for the South train, and now I shall have to wait another five minutes for the Tarnforth, I suppose. Ah !

here she is," as a short train appeared round the curve of a little branch line, and ran into the other side of the station.

A few moments more, and, with a parting jerk of the hand from each driver, both trains were off almost simultaneously, there being but two passengers from Tarnforth for Morton's train, and none for the other.

" What was that you were asking him about a bank ?" inquired Gerard, as soon as they were well under weigh again.

" Oh, it's a heavy incline up Mosshope Fell, about six miles from here," replied Morton. " We call inclines banks, and there's always a pilot or bank engine waiting to give a shove up to any train that wants it. But the old gentleman says it's all right, and we've got a light train, so we shall run up alone. Sometimes, when the rails are slippery, and with a heavy train, it's an awful business. Mind yourself, Zeke's going to fire up again."

On they sped again through the wild moorland. The moon had quite risen by this time, and the view, as they got into a still wilder and more rugged country, was picturesque in the extreme. The air, too, became keener and

keener, and Gerard turned up his coat collar,
and was glad to get as much shelter as was
afforded by the weather-board. They stopped
at a small station a few miles farther on, and
after this all signs of human life or habitation
seemed to disappear altogether.

"There's the bank-engine waiting," observed
Morton, as they started again, and passed an
engine with steam up, waiting in a siding.
"All right to-night, Peter," he called out to
the driver, a burly individual with a huge red
beard, who was standing on the ground near
his engine, but stepped across the rails and
mounted on to Morton's as the train slowly
moved off; "shan't want you to-night; old
Elijah says the bank travels well, and my
train's very light."

"Ay, ay," rejoined Peter, "ye'll get up
fine; but there'll be the goods behind ye will
need me, I'm thinking. Eh! but it's just a
bonny night, and ye'll see the whole country
fra' the top o' Summit;" and, watching his
opportunity, he swung himself off on to the
ground with a wave of his hand, and was soon
left behind.

Another mile or two, and they were beginning the ascent of Mosshope Bank, a steep incline of about three miles on one side, with a gradual descent of some six or seven on the other. More steam was applied, and the engine puffed away vigorously, but the speed of the train began to be considerably reduced, and Gerard could feel that the work was now "against the collar." Still, the rails were pretty dry and the train light, so they jogged steadily up at a very serviceable sort of pace ; and the reduced speed enabled Gerard to have a little more connected conversation with the driver.

"I say, George, old boy," he began, " you know this game of yours beats me altogether. It's the queerest thing I ever heard of ; and I can't make it out even now. How do you manage with the other drivers and fellows, for instance ? I should have thought they wouldn't have cared about a chap like you coming in among them in this sort of way."

" Oh, there's not much bother about that," replied the other. " They know I'm only on a temporary job, and that sort of thing is often done. There are fellows who want to qualify for something—railway berths in the

colonies, and that sort of thing—and they come
on as firemen or drivers for a bit, just to learn
the practical part of the business. Of course
one must be a regular engineer, though, and
have been through the shops and all that sort
of thing; they won't have any humbug about
it. But, you see, I did all that some time
ago; and these fellows think I'm just quali-
fying too. Of course I had to begin as a fireman, so as to learn the road, and the signals,
and all the rest of it. I fired with old Elijah
Wilson for nearly two months, and have only
been driving this last week; in fact, I ought
by rights to be still firing now."

"Well, it's a rum go, anyway," remarked
Gerard. "I say though, George, it's beastly
selfish of me to be always thinking about
myself. There's something wrong with you
too, or you wouldn't be at this business.
Anything I can do for you, old chap? I
wish you'd tell me."

"Never mind me, Jerry, my boy," replied
Morton, lighting his pipe. "I'm a queer sort
of fellow, you know; and I won't say that I
haven't got my troubles, like most other
people. Perhaps I'll tell you some day;

"but just now I'm all for being let alone,
you understand ; and you know me too well
to mind that.   Perhaps I may turn up again
in London before long ; but, anyhow, if you
want to write to me, a letter will always reach
me in course of time, if you write to the old
place.   I'm living at Starlington just now ;
but, you see, I've got another name when
I'm driving.   If ever you really wanted to
find me quick, you must write to George
Adams, 7 Railway Buildings, Starlington,
where I stop when I'm off the road.   But I'd
just as soon keep quiet there, you understand,
and the other place would find me right
enough."

"All right, old boy," returned Gerard ; "I
quite understand ; but I do hope it will come
all right some day—all right for both of us," he
added, with a sigh, "though I can't say I feel
very hopeful about myself.   But I'm awfully
glad to have seen you, anyhow, old man ; and
it's an immense relief to me to have been able
to tell you all about it."

"Ah, Jerry," replied Morton, "if only my
business could be as easily settled as I expect
yours will be, I shouldn't think much about

it. I'll just tell you one thing, though, old
fellow. Don't have any nonsense about it,
and be sure you know your own mind, or by
G—d," he added, in a voice that startled
Gerard by its stern tone of warning, " you'll
be sorry for it some day. Now hold on hard,
as we're over Summit, and shall go down the
other side like blazes."

They had now reached the top of the incline, or " summit," according to railway
phraseology, indicated by a lonely little signal-
box, a siding, and a rough water apparatus
rising on piles out of a deep pool by the side
of the rails, and looking like a gigantic beacon
in a ridiculously small sea. The driver of the
bank engine had not gone beyond the truth
when he spoke of the view to be obtained
from this eminence. A wide expanse of hill
country stretched far away on all sides ; here
a sharp edge standing out clear in the moonlight, there a glen or valley shrouded in deep
mysterious shadows which gave a fantastic
and unreal appearance to everything around.
The hills were not as a rule steep or precipi-
tous ; but there was a peculiar grandeur and
dignity in the rolling sea of moorland and fell

that stretched away in an apparently bound-
less succession of wave-like ridges, which in
the uncertain moonlight had the appearance
of being far more mountainous than they
really were.

"By Jove, what a lovely night!" exclaimed
Gerard, steadying himself against the weather-
board; for they had begun the descent of the
incline, and although all steam had been shut
off, they were gliding down at what seemed a
terrific pace. "It's worth anything to have
seen this," he continued; "hang it! I wish I
was an engine-driver!"

"Ah, it's all very well on a fine night like
this," rejoined Morton, slightly altering the
position of a lever, "but it's quite another
thing in rough weather. Some of these poor
chaps have a real bad time of it now and
then, I can tell you. But I'm glad it's so
fine to-night, as you're here, and this is an
uncommon pretty run, to be sure."

So they skimmed along, almost noiselessly,
with a mysterious, unaccountable sort of
motion that was very fascinating, now round-
ing a corner of some dark hill, now skirting
the edge of a shadowy valley, and now rumb-

ling over some little mountain stream ; but
all the time evidently getting towards lower
ground. They flashed past one or two
desolate little stations, and then evident
preparations were made for a stoppage.
Morton made a quick sign to the fireman, who
commenced to work the brake vigorously,
and himself looked over the side and towards
the rear of the train, as if to take an observation.

"Stop at Mosshopefoot," he said to Gerard,
"and have to begin to pull up three miles off,
it's such an incline. We've come these last
five miles without any steam at all, you see.
Haven't got the continuous brakes on this part
of the line yet, but we want them uncommonly
here."

After leaving Mosshopefoot, the aspect of
the country became quite different, the line
now running through a wide valley or strath
alongside of a fair-sized stream ; and in another ten minutes they had begun to slacken
speed for Bellmoor, the station whither Gerard
was bound.

"Well, Jerry, my boy," said Morton, as
they ran into the station, "we must part

company here.   I'm awfully glad to have
seen you and had a chat about things.   Perhaps I'll see you again soon, perhaps not ;
anyhow, you know where to write if you
really want anything.   Good-bye now, and
God bless you."   And as if anxious to avoid
any further farewell, he grasped his oil-can,
and swinging himself over the side, almost
before the engine had stopped, began to
busy himself among the machinery.   And
in five minutes more Gerard and his traps
were in the dog - cart that had been sent
to meet him, and on the road to Bellmoor
Lodge.

CHAPTER XXIV.

RETROSPECTIVE.

It has often been remarked—and by some, moreover, who may be considered as fairly qualified to express an opinion on the subject —that there is no direct advantage in telling a lie when the object desired may be as readily attained by speaking the truth. Similarly, we hold that the cordial relations which ought to exist between author and reader are not likely to be in any way enhanced by the keeping up of a mystery when there is no necessity for so doing. And as the main thread of our narrative is in no way affected by the previous history of George Morton, we think that it may be just as well to take our readers into our confidence at once, and enlighten them as to the motives, without some explanation of which that gentleman's conduct, as described in the preceding chapter and elsewhere, might appear somewhat unaccountable.

We will, then, crave indulgence for a moment's delay in the course of our story, and take a retrospective glance at a little episode in George Morton's life which occurred some five or six years before his first introduction to them in connection with Gerard Courtenay.

The scene is an old-fashioned rectory garden in one of the south-western counties. A trim lawn slopes down to a pretty trout-stream, which a hundred yards higher up ripples lazily over gravelly shallows, where in the heat of the day the cattle may be heard splashing about up to their knees in the cool water, but is here confined in a narrower and deeper channel between moss-grown old brick walls, and flows on in a steady, business-like current under the dark shadow of a grey old wooden bridge, towards the mill-dam on the left, where, behind a luxuriant cluster of evergreens, the white-washed gables and red-tiled roof of the mill stand up against the clear blue sky. On the right is a shrubbery reaching down to the water, backed by a cluster of elms, where a colony of rooks are holding a noisy conclave. Behind is the rectory house, a low, two-storied stone building, the sober colouring of which is relieved by a bright band of flower - beds stretching along the entire front; while above all rises the grey church tower, round which the jackdaws are doing their best to emulate the clamour of the rooks in the adjoining elms.

It is a lovely morning in June; and even at this early hour—for the clock in the old church tower has only just struck seven—both house and garden are bathed in a flood of brilliant sunshine. There is as yet little sign of life indoors, and the blinds are still down in most of the windows. Early as is the hour, however, it does not appear to be thought unseasonable by two persons who are strolling along the little gravel walk by the stream, and apparently engrossed in a most interesting conversation. As the clock strikes, one of them, a tall, good-looking young man of about five-and-twenty, utters an exclamation of impatience and regret, and pulls out his watch as if to dispute the time with the church. They are now at the end of the wall by the little bridge, and screened from observation by a mass of evergreens. He

turns about abruptly, and stands face to face
with his companion.

It is not, indeed, wonderful that he should
be loth to quit the society in which he finds
himself; for a fairer specimen of an English
girl than Constance Molyneux it would at
that time have been difficult to find. She
was considerably above the middle height, and
had a way of holding her head that made her
appear still taller.   But, tall as she was, it
would have been a fastidious critic who could
have found fault with the lines of her graceful
undulating figure, while the well-shaped,
queenly little head and full, rounded throat
would have afforded a model for a sculptor.
The mouth was perhaps a trifle too large for
strict beauty, but it was easy to overlook such
a trifling defect, if indeed it could be called
such, when combined with the loveliest violet
eyes imaginable, and with a freshness and
delicacy of colouring that it would have been
difficult to surpass. As she stands there, this
June morning, in a simple white muslin dress,
just relieved by a crimson rose-bud, and an
old straw hat stuck carelessly on a mass of
dark-brown hair, one or two little rebellious

locks of which have straggled down on to her fair forehead, she is a bright and sunny picture —such a picture indeed of youth and freshness, as yet unsullied by the sorrows and disappointments of the world, as it does one good to look upon.

"I must be off, I suppose," says her companion, with a sigh ; "one must allow three-quarters of an hour to catch the train, and that old fly-horse doesn't look as if he would care much about being hurried."

"Yes, I suppose you ought to be going," she replies, with just the slightest possible change of colour ; "I hope you will have a pleasant journey, and you must let us hear of you again some day."

"Ah, Constance," he exclaims, "will you care to hear about me, I wonder?" and he seizes her hand in both of his.

"Well, perhaps I may," she replies, with a lovely blush, but drawing her hand gently away. "Now, you must really be off. What will papa say when he hears I got up to see you off like this?"

"Won't you give me that rose," he pleads, regardless of papa's problematical displeasure, "just as a remembrance of this morning? not that I require anything to remind me of you, you know, but still"——

She takes the rose-bud slowly from her breast, but hesitates a moment before giving it him. "There, take it, and be off," she at length says, hurriedly. One more pressure of the hand, and in another moment he has disappeared behind the evergreens.

All very pretty and romantic, no doubt, we fancy we hear the reader say. Young man staying at rectory—falls in love with rector's pretty daughter—love marriage and all the rest of it.

Such, unquestionably, would be the natural and orthodox sequel to this little summer idyl. As, however, things in this world do not invariably turn out exactly as we consider that we have a right to expect, we must ask our readers to imagine that a period of eighteen months has elapsed, and once again take a glance at the rectory garden.

It is a chill afternoon in December. The old house looks damp and cheerless, and a bleak wintry wind is moaning through the bare branches of the elms, and whisking the

dead leaves across the sodden lawn. Heavy
rains have swollen and discoloured the little
stream, which has here and there overflowed
its boundaries and formed standing pools on
the gravel walk. An occasional shuddering
gust of wind sweeps across the dull, leaden
water, now almost up to the floor of the
wooden bridge ; and a water-rat, essaying to
cross to a hole on the other side, finds it as
much as he can do to make headway against
the current. Everything, in fact, looks gloomy
and depressing, and suggestive of the rapidly
waning year.

At the corner by the bridge two persons
are standing, whom it is not difficult to recognise as the same from whom we parted
at the same spot that lovely morning in
June. But eighteen months have wrought
a sad change in one of them. The brilliant
colouring has departed ; the face looks pale
and thin ; and there are dark circles round
those violet eyes that speak unmistakably
of care and sorrow. Nothing could ever
make Constance Molyneux appear otherwise
than graceful and highbred ; but even that
slim, lissome figure has now a drooping look

about it; and as she draws her waterproof
cloak more closely round her to protect her
dress from a shower of moisture that a gust
of wind has driven off the evergreens, it is
painfully evident that she is not the same
bright creature who stood there in the June
sunshine only a short eighteen months ago.

The lapse of time does not appear to have
much affected her companion. He is young
and comely as ever; and there are no traces
of care or anxiety about his handsome face.
But there is a look upon it that it is not
altogether pleasant to see—a look of shame
contending with selfishness, in a struggle
where selfishness has obtained the mastery.
His head is bent down, and he is boring little
holes with his stick in the damp gravel. His
general demeanour is, in fact, very different
from what it was that bright morning in June,
and the contrast is hardly to his advantage.

The last time we saw them here, they had
plenty to say to each other. Now, however,
the conversation seems to flag, and they are
both apparently oppressed by a feeling of
restraint and uneasiness. At last, however,
she speaks.

" I suppose we shall not see anything more of you at present ? " she says, in a voice that is intended to be unconcerned, but in which it is possible to detect a slight tremor.

" No ; I'm afraid not," he replies. " I don't know exactly how long I shall be away ; but I don't expect to be home again much before this time next year."

His voice, too, is somewhat constrained and unnatural, though he affects an appearance of indifference. The situation is, in fact, very far from being comfortable, and it is evident that the relations of the parties towards each other have become just a little strained.

There is another uncomfortable pause, which, however, is interrupted by the striking of the old church clock. Miss Molyneux draws her waterproof round her with a slight shiver, and looks her companion steadily in the face.

" You are going by the four o'clock train, are you not ? " she says ; " you must not let me keep you here."

He, too, looks up in her face for a moment, but, somehow or other, is unable to meet the glance of those sweet violet eyes, that seem to

look through and through him. "Yes, I must
be off," he replies in a sort of half-defiant, half-
desperate tone; and then, as if still inclined
to linger, "I'm so sorry not to have seen your
father. I do hope he will get all right again
soon."

"Thanks," she answers coldly; "I am afraid
he won't be about again for a long time yet.
But you mustn't lose your train; don't you
think you ought to be going?" and she holds
out her hand, as if to wish him good-bye.

He takes it in his, but still lingers on,
though he dares not look in her face again.
"Good-bye," at length he says, in a hoarse
whisper, and, with one last pressure of her
hand, he is gone, and she is once more standing there alone.

"Well," the reader will very likely say,
"there is nothing very remarkable in all this.
They have had a quarrel perhaps, and will of
course make it up again; but surely there is
nothing to make a fuss about."

No; it is nothing to make a fuss about,
perhaps, and it represents a by no means
unusual occurrence in everyday life. It can
hardly be described as a quarrel, however. It

is simply this, that the gentleman has changed his mind, while the lady, curiously enough, remains the same.

So George Morton went on his way, and, Constance Molyneux remained at the old rectory, to think over the past and nurse her father, who had been in failing health for some months past. He was an old man, and had held the living of Under Newton for nearly forty years; but until lately had been hale and vigorous as any man of his age in the parish. He had caught a chill, however, during the preceding summer, which, through being neglected, had resulted in congestion of the lungs; and though he had in a certain measure recovered, he had never regained his strength, and there were threatenings of other complications of a still more serious nature. In the mean time he was entirely confined to his room, and the affairs of the parish were left in the hands of his curate. It had been a sad time, therefore, for Constance, his only child, who had long had the cares of their small household upon her, and who was now burdened with the additional charge of a sick father.

Miss Molyneux had led a quiet and uneventful life at the old rectory till within the last two years. Her mother had died when she was quite a child, and it had never occurred to her father, a man of a stay-at-home and indolent disposition, that it was either necessary or desirable for his daughter to see more of the world than was to be found in the neighbourhood of Under Newton. And a quieter corner of England it would have been difficult to imagine. It was a thinly populated district, with few resident gentry, and the nearest town of any importance a good fifteen miles away; and though of late years a branch railway had been opened which had brought Under Newton within five miles of a little roadside station, no great impetus appeared to have been thereby given either to social or commercial interests. Society, in fact, according to modern ideas, there was none, and most persons who should be called upon to pass their days at Under Newton would have considered themselves as to all intents and purposes shut out from the world. But even in this out-of-the-way corner of the kingdom there were one or two houses here and

there whose owners, when at home, endeavoured
manfully to do their duty to society as far as
in them lay; and it was at a lawn-tennis
party at one of these, where George Morton
happened to be staying, that he first met
Constance Molyneux. It was not wonderful,
perhaps, that he should have been attracted by
her; and it was not long before he was introduced to her father, and obtained a footing
in her home. People in these out-of-the-way
parts of the country are generally somewhat
unsophisticated, and given to hospitality in
regard to chance visitors. George Morton
soon found out that there was good trout-
fishing to be had near Under Newton; and
although he took up his quarters in the
most innocent manner at the village inn,
it was only natural that after a few days
they should be transferred to the rectory.
And after this, the result was only what
might have been expected.

And yet there had been no positive engagement, no plighted vows—nothing, in fact,
that in a lower grade of life could have been
worked up into a case for breach of promise.
But every one knew that Constance Molyneux

had been jilted, and she herself knew only too well that she had given away her heart, and had got nothing in return.

Misfortunes seldom, if ever, come alone. The old rector, whose strength had been gradually declining, became rapidly worse, and before the new year he was lying in the churchyard. George Morton was by this time far away from England, and remained in ignorance of the old man's death. The next intelligence he received of Constance Molyneux was the announcement, which he happened to see in an English paper at San Francisco some six months later, of her marriage to Augustus Caledon, Esq., of H.B.M. Consular Service.

Morton's first, and not very unnatural reflection, was that the lady had not lost much time in consoling herself. It was not the first time he had heard of Mr Caledon, who, like himself, had been staying in that part of the country, and whom the same attraction had drawn to the rectory. It had been evident to every one that he, too, had admired Miss Molyneux; but George Morton, in the pride of five-and-twenty, had never looked upon a man of fifty or thereabouts as a serious rival,

and had not even contemplated the possibility
of his being accepted as a suitor. The news
was therefore something of a shock to him,
especially as during the last month or so his
thoughts had in the most unaccountable manner again reverted to the love which he had
taught himself to look upon as an idle fancy,
and of which he had long since thought himself entirely cured. Human nature is, however, proverbially inconsistent; and it was
not, perhaps, to be wondered at that George
Morton, who had certainly for the moment
been very much in love with Constance Molyneux, more, perhaps, than he had any idea of,
should have experienced a kind of reaction
when he found that she had altogether
passed away from him, and that the old feeling should have returned upon him with ten-
fold power. He tried to persuade himself
that it was all for the best, and that her proceedings could no longer be a matter of any
possible interest to him. But, somehow or
other, he could not get her out of his head,
and he began to detest Augustus Caledon,
Esq., of H.B.M. Consular Service, with all
his heart.

Without going further into the history of George Morton's resuscitated affection, it will be sufficient to say that, within a month of his seeing the announcement of Constance's marriage, he was more in love with her than ever, and, alas! with that hopeless, desperate passion that, when once it has entered into a man's heart, leaves little room for anything else. He was travelling with a friend at the time, and had some thoughts of turning his face towards England, but, after this intelligence, the idea of coming home seemed hateful to him, and he was easily persuaded to accompany his friend on a further expedition likely to last some months longer. He returned home at last, cured, as he thought, and with the determination to dismiss Constance for ever from his thoughts. But it was not long before some trifling incident brought everything back to him, and within two months of his return he was in a worse state than ever.

So things went on with Morton for about a year, during which time he was subject to alternations of the deepest depression and self-reproach, and of a sort of listlessness that, while to all appearance it did not prevent his going on much as usual, seemed to take all the brightness out of his life, and to render him indifferent to almost everything that went on around him. He had heard nothing whatever of Constance, and had not even attempted to learn any news of her. But he was roused one day from this state of apathy by another newspaper announcement of a nature that he had little anticipated. Once more his eye was caught by a name that was now painfully familiar to him, and with dizzy brain and a scarcely beating heart he read of the sudden death of Augustus Caledon, Esq., H.B.M. Consul at Augsburg, aged fifty-three.

His first impulse was to rush off to Augsburg at once, and throw himself at her feet. Then he reflected that such a proceeding on his part would seem to her utterly unreasonable and inconsistent, and that if, as he had every reason to suppose, she had got over any feelings of affection she might once have had for him, it would hardly be the way most calculated to win them back. No, he must allow a certain time to elapse, and then approach her by degrees. But the mere fact

of her being once more free, in a manner too
that he never dared to think of or hope for,
seemed to give him new life, and he set himself to wait as patiently as he could till such
time as he felt he could with ordinary decency
venture to bring himself once more to her
notice.

It would not seem a very difficult task, at
the present day, to follow or trace out the
movements of a person who has occupied a
tolerably prominent position in a minor Con-
tinental town.　Morton never had the smallest
doubt of being able to find out Mrs Caledon
whenever the proper moment should arrive,
by the simple process of making inquiries at
Augsburg, whence, supposing she had left
the place after her husband's death, it
would be easy to trace her to wherever she
might have retired.　In this theory he was
supported by a friend at the International
Office, who assured him that there would be
no trouble whatever about it, and undertook
to make confidential inquiries through the
acting consul.　It was with some surprise,
therefore, not to say perturbation, that Morton was informed by his friend, some ten

days later, that Mrs Caledon had left Augsburg
the day after her husband's funeral, accompanied only by her own maid, and leaving
behind her neither address nor indeed any
trace whatever. The other servants had been
paid off and dismissed ; and no one in Augsburg had the slightest idea what had become
of her, beyond the bare fact that she had left
by a certain train going in the direction of
Frankfort.

This intelligence was by no means encouraging ; but Morton endeavoured to console himself by the reflection that it was impossible
that she should have left absolutely no trace
behind her, and that it only required the
presence of some one really in earnest to hit
off the scent. He was beginning to get restless and impatient beyond endurance ; so
without more ado he put himself into the
train, and went straight to Augsburg, determined to investigate matters thoroughly for
himself. But he soon found to his dismay
that his diplomatic friend had been perfectly
right, and that Mrs Caledon had vanished
without leaving the very slightest trace behind her. So well concealed, indeed, had

been her movements, that it seemed evident
that an intentional secrecy had been observed.
He succeeded in ascertaining that a lady
answering to her description had taken tickets
for Paris ; but this was in itself too slender a
thread of evidence to constitute a clue of any
importance ; and after three or four days
spent in fruitless inquiries, he returned to
England no wiser than when he started.

It would be too tedious to follow George
Morton through all his experiences in search
of his lost love.   But at the end of six months,
during which time he had, as he thought,
exhausted every conceivable means of getting
on her track, he was as ignorant of her whereabouts as ever.   It is true that he had not
much to go upon ; for the only other place
besides Augsburg where he could reasonably
hope for a clue was her old home at Under
Newton.   But here his researches resulted in
an absolute blank.   It appeared that Miss
Molyneux had left almost directly after her
father's death ; his successor was entirely un-
acquainted with her ; and the most that could
be gathered from the natives of the village
was that she had written to one or two old

people with whom she had been particularly intimate, to announce her marriage and the fact that she was about to go abroad. Since then, nothing had been heard about her; and there was absolutely nothing therefore upon which to found an inquiry.

It is extremely probable that if Morton had placed the affair in the hands of a private detective, it would not have been long before some clue had been obtained of Mrs Caledon's whereabouts. But he could not quite bring himself to resort to such an expedient. Conscious, all too late, of having behaved very badly to her, he shrank instinctively from taking a step that, if discovered, she might justly resent as an unwarrantable impertinence; and determined, though with a despairing heart, that, if she was to be found, it must be by his own individual exertions. Once or twice, indeed, he fancied that he had come upon her track; but his hopes were on each occasion doomed to disappointment, and after each failure he became more despondent than ever. It was on one of these occasions that, sick and weary of his desultory existence, he suddenly resolved to endeavour to

escape from himself and the bitter contemplation of the past by embarking in some occupation that would demand hard and continuous labour, both mental and physical. His
engineering education here stood him in good
stead. He obtained through a friend an
introduction to a director of one of the leading northern lines; was passed on by him
to the locomotive superintendent, and having proved satisfactorily that he possessed a
competent knowledge of the most important
details of engine-work, was taken on as a
fireman, from which humble position he was
soon raised to that of an extra driver. And
this is how Gerard Courtenay ran up against
him at Long Heaton Junction.

CHAPTER XXV.

"THERE WAS NO DOUBT ABOUT IT?"

"LORD BALLYBRACK, will you take Lady Adelaide? Colonel Scott, will you take Miss Sartoris? I'm so sorry I've no young lady for you, Gerard; but come and sit by me, and tell me all about yourself." And having thus spoken, the Countess of Mount Easton gave her arm to the Earl of Narborough, and rustled after her guests into the dining-room.

Bellmoor Lodge was not a large house, and incapable therefore of accommodating any great number of visitors, especially if all the younger members of the family happened to be at home. There was nominally room for three married couples, and when the boys were at school, for four or five bachelor guests, one of whom might possibly be called upon to sleep in a bathroom, which had been fitted up to do duty as a bedroom at a pinch. The house had originally, as its name implied,

been only a shooting-lodge, but had by degrees been added and added to until it had
attained its present dimensions. The fine air
and general healthiness of the locality had
caused it to be selected from among the
numerous residences of the Marquis of St.
Ives as the abode of the Mount Eastons and
their youthful family ; and there was a talk
every year of adding a new wing, or otherwise
enlarging the house. But somehow or other
the projected operations never came off, and
it remained an ugly, inconvenient, and yet
thoroughly homelike and lovable old house, to
which all members of the family were much
attached.

At the present moment the house was as
full as it could hold, even down to the bathroom, which had been assigned to Gerard, and
which was in reality far more comfortable
than its designation implied, having been con-
verted by fresh chintzes, a luxurious arm-chair,
and other minor appliances, into what was in
fact an ordinary bedroom, with the addition
of a huge fixed bath. The fire-place was
certainly somewhat peculiar, having been
originally a closed stove, and designed more

for utility than ornament; but it gave out
plenty of heat, which was the great point
after all ; and a wearied sportsman, returning
after a long tramp over the hills or a day's
covert-shooting along the steep wooded banks
of the Bell or Beil Water, is not as a rule
disposed to criticise the design of the fireplace
in his bedroom, as long as the fire itself is
bright and cheerful.

The party consisted of Lord and Lady
Narborough, and Lady Adelaide, Lord Narborough's sister, whom we have met before;
our old friend the "Cadger;" Colonel Scott
of Newlands Castle, about fifteen miles distant; Miss Sartoris, a connection of the
family; a guardsman cousin of Lady Mount
Easton's ; a sailor brother of his lordship's ;
and our hero.

The Earl of Narborough was a stout, estimable young man of about five-and-thirty,
though in appearance and manner he might
have passed for some years older. He was
one of those persons respecting whom, though
blameless to the last degree in the position to
which they have been called, it is impossible
not to wonder how it is that Providence has

not assigned them some other walk in life. He would have made a fair curate or a tolerable missionary, and had destiny and his own inclinations so willed it, he was by no means destitute of such talents as, combined with a tractable disposition and regular habits, might have enabled him to attain a respectable position in the Civil Service. But a casual observer, meeting him in mixed society, would never for a moment have supposed that he was the head of a noble and ancient family, and the tenant for life of one of the finest properties in the south of England. His outward appearance was certainly not in his favour, for he was somewhat below middle height, with a decided tendency to corpulence, and although his features were good and his expression not unpleasant, his movements were awkward and ungainly, and it was seldom that he really appeared at his ease. Add to this a self-conscious, nervous, and rather peevish manner, with a tendency to stammer, and it will readily be understood that the tenth Earl of Narborough did not altogether come up to the generally accepted definition of a popular man. And yet it must be confessed, that whatever faults he had were chiefly external and superficial, for a more well-intentioned and conscientious creature never existed.

But however small an opinion the world might have of the social qualities of the noble earl, there was but one opinion as to the lady whom he had been so fortunate as to secure as his wife. Sensible, good-natured, gifted with a keen sense of humour, and at the same time an inexhaustible fund of patience and a happy disposition that never seemed ruffled by her husband's little caprices and weaknesses, she managed him as probably very few others could have done; and those who had known him before his marriage were compelled to admit that he had very much improved since. It had in fact been a matter of some speculation whether his lordship would ever marry, for from the time of his coming of age he had been deeply impressed with the idea that he was the one central object of attraction to the mothers of England, and that every young lady he met had matrimonial designs upon him. It is quite probable that his apprehensions on this subject were in many cases far from groundless; but at the same time, and although unquestionably a first-class *parti*, he was not, as he appeared to think, the only rich young heir to a peerage in the matrimonial market; and after three or four seasons, during which the attractions of various eligible young ladies had been in vain paraded before him, it began to be said that he was not likely to marry; and one or two mammas had even been heard to declare that nothing should induce them to allow their darlings to risk their happiness with such a man. It is within the limits of possibility that these good ladies might have already tried their hands on his lordship without success; but be this as it may, he began to be looked upon as of little account; and his own tastes not leading him much into society, the danger into which he imagined himself to be perpetually exposed became less and less every year. At the same time, his apprehensions on this score were not in any way diminished, and nothing in the world would have induced him to remain alone in a room for five minutes with any young person who by any stretch of imagination could have been considered as a possible candidate for the honour of a matrimonial alliance. So time rolled on, till one day some astonishment was created in fashionable circles by the announcement of his engagement to Miss Brabazon, the eldest daughter of a west-country baronet, with a limited rent-roll and a large family, who had scarcely ever been seen in London, and whose name had never been connected with his lordship's in any way.

This intelligence may have caused certain mothers to regret that they had not followed up the pursuit of the noble earl a little closer; and much speculation was for the moment excited as to the nature of the circumstances which could have induced him to make up his mind to propose. Public interest in the matter, however, soon died out; and Lord Easthampton, as he then was, and his wife very soon settled down into a respectable and domestic country couple, only appearing in London on rare occasions, and of very little account in the fashionable world. They had now been married about five years, in the course of which time his lordship had succeeded to the family honours, and having been presented with two girls, his mind, which had hitherto been much exercised on the subject, had at length been relieved by the appearance of a son and heir.

The shooting at Bellmoor, though not affording the opportunities for slaughter which are considered by many modern sportsmen a *sine quâ non*, was very good of its kind, and especially enjoyable by reason of the nature of the ground and the lovely scenery; and as Gerard settled himself comfortably before the fire after his first day's sport, and prepared for half an hour's doze before dressing for dinner, he felt as if the world were not such a very bad place after all. He had had a very pleasant day, and was just comfortably tired; the change of air and exercise had already done him good; and he always felt more or less happy when in the company of Lady Mount Easton. Then there was his other cousin, too, or reputed cousin, Adelaide Middleton, who was always very nice, and whom he was glad to see again; and that Miss Sartoris seemed a good sort of girl too. Altogether, our friend Gerard felt somehow that as far as present and external circumstances went he had not much to complain of; and although the thought of his far-away love

and of the uncertainty and hoplessness that
seemed to surround his prospects was ever
present to him, and would at times absorb
everything else, the elasticity of youth, and
a naturally buoyant and happy disposition,
enabled him to cast his cares to a great extent
on one side, and to forget for the time all
thought of the future in the enjoyment of the
present.

"Rum fellow Narborough," observed the
"Cadger," as he seated himself in an arm-
chair in the smoking-room that evening. It
is hardly necessary to observe that the nobleman thus referred to was not present, one of
his little peculiarities being a rooted aversion
to tobacco in any shape or form. "D——d
dangerous shot too," he continued ; "shot at
a rabbit right between us, and the shot came
all round me. Ain't sure he didn't hit me, by
Gad," feeling tenderly down one leg, "or else
it's a d——d big thorn."

"By Jove, you don't say so !" exclaimed
Lord Mount Easton, lighting a cigar at the
fire. "I say, let's undress the old Cadger,
and see if he's really been hit. We'll soon
pick it out, old chap ; here's a knife with a

pair of tweezers in it; or if that won't do, we'll try a corkscrew."

This proposal was received with acclamation by all except the individual immediately concerned, who showed no signs of a desire to be operated upon in the manner suggested; and after the pretence of a scuffle with Lord Mount Easton, who approached with a knife in one hand and a corkscrew in the other, the party settled down comfortably in various attitudes of repose, and smoking soon became general.

"Hang it all, though," observed Mount Easton, more seriously, "I'm afraid he is rather dangerous. He don't seem particular where he points his gun, and I'll take my oath he let it off once by accident. He pretended he was shooting at a rabbit in some thick stuff, but I was near him, and I'll swear he never got his gun up to his shoulder. However, we'll put him well on the left to-morrow, and keep him there; and if he shoots you again, Cadger, old boy, why, just you let him have it back, you know."

"Oh, yes, that's all devilish fine," responded the "Cadger," gloomily. "I wish he'd stay

at home, though. What the deuce can he
want to go out shooting for? He can't hit
a haystack, and he don't seem much of a
hand at walking either. He's a rum beggar
altogether; can't say I care much about
him."

"Oh, he's not half a bad chap, really, when
you get to know him," said Mount Easton.
"He always was a muff, you know, and never
could do anything like any one else; but
he's a good-hearted sort of fellow, and he
isn't half such a fool as he looks, I can tell
you."

"Well, that's devilish lucky," broke in the
guardsman, "for he's one of the stupidest
fellows to look at I ever saw. But isn't there
something odd in the family? Father was a
rum un too, wasn't he?"

"No, no, my dear Bill," said Mount Easton;
"why, his father was a dear old boy,—best
fellow in the world, though a bit pig-headed.
Used to pitch into this chap like anything
for being such a muff. Awful pity he's dead;
and he wasn't really an old man, either. No;
you're thinking of his uncle, whom his father
succeeded; he was rather off his head, I

believe, and came to an end in some extraordinary way."

"Ah, well," interposed the veteran Colonel
Scott, who had not as yet taken any part in
the conversation, "I'm not so sure about
that either. Of course it was long before the
time of any of you; but I remember him very
well, and he was just as fine a young fellow
as ever lived. It was a most extraordinary
case, but I don't believe that there was really
anything wrong with him. He had simply
got it into his head that he would improve
himself and all that sort of thing by seeing
the world as a working man, and I've no
doubt whatever," knocking the ashes off his
cigar, "that if only he had lived, poor fellow,
he would have had something to show for it.
Your father was a great friend of his, I recollect," turning to Gerard, "and I've no doubt
you have heard him speak of him."

"What happened to him, then?" inquired
the "Cadger," sleepily. "Oh, ah, by the way,
I remember now. Blown up in one of those
d——d river steamers in America, wasn't
he?"

"No," replied Colonel Scott; "he wasn't

exactly blown up, but he got scalded by an escape of steam or something, and died two or three days afterwards. He was working as a common sailor, or boatman, or something of that kind, at the time, and you can imagine the excitement over there when they found out who he was."

"I suppose there was no doubt about it, was there?" inquired Mount Easton. "I mean, that it really was him who was killed. I fancy I've heard people say that the evidence was supposed to be a bit doubtful, and that there was some danger of a claimant turning up, or something of the kind."

"Oh, no," replied the Colonel, "I fancy it was all clear enough. There was only one of the law lords, or whoever they were, who had to decide, who had any doubt about it, and that was only old Brentford, who never would agree with anybody. Besides, it's over forty years ago now, and if there had been a claimant to come forward, we should have heard about it long ago."

"Ah, well," observed Mount Easton, "I wish this chap's father had lived. Why, he wasn't much over sixty when he died, though he looked older. It was that fall that did it; he was always fooling about with young horses, and thought he could break them himself, and one day he got rolled over and regularly smashed up."

"Well, this sportsman won't kill himself that way, anyhow," remarked the guardsman; "he never gets outside a horse by any chance, does he?"

"No, I fancy not," replied Mount Easton, helping himself to some whisky and potashwater. "Well, you fellows, I'm going to bed; and mind, breakfast at eight sharp to-morrow. Cadger, you'd better go to bed too, or you won't be up in time." So his lordship disappeared, and the party shortly afterwards broke up, and retired to their well-earned repose.

CHAPTER XXVI.

"WHERE DID YOU GET THAT BROOCH?"

THE next day's shooting was near the house, and the sportsmen, on their return, found themselves with a couple of hours to spare before dinner. There was accordingly a general gathering in the library, and a considerable run upon the tea-table and its accompaniments. There is no time, by the way, when male society is, to all appearances, more welcome to the fair sex than the hour of afternoon tea. Perhaps it is that the ladies have by this time had enough of each other's society, and the usual feminine topics of discussion have been completely exhausted. Or possibly our fair enslavers may be thoroughly aware of the fact that there is no moment when they appear more charming in the eyes of their admirers than when the latter have just returned, wet and tired, from the pursuit of some out-door sport. The sudden transition from a cold, stormy night out-of-doors to the warmth and luxury of a lady's boudoir certainly affords about as great a contrast as could well be imagined; and the ministering angel who offers you a cup of tea, appears, under such circumstances, to be very few degrees removed from a *houri* of paradise.

Be this as it may, however, there was a very cheery party in the library at Bellmoor that evening, and a good deal of pleasant chaff and repartee was flying about. The " Cadger," although undoubtedly a "parti" as far as his position and title went, whatever doubts might have been entertained as to the resources of the Ballybrack property, was not generally looked upon as a marrying man, and had in fact begun to be regarded in many quarters as an incurable bachelor. But he was always popular with women, whether actuated by matrimonial designs upon him or not, and his good-natured and easy-going disposition made up for other little shortcomings. On the present occasion he was in great force, being, as he himself expressed it, a "nailer" at tea and bread-and-butter, with which refresh-

ments he was being assiduously supplied by
Lady Adelaide and Miss Sartoris, to both of
whom he was pretending to make desperate
love, without, however, conveying any very
strong impression of the sincerity of his pro-
fessions. That excellent young nobleman, the
Earl of Narborough, was holding forth at
length to Lady Mount Easton, a cup of tea
in one hand and a piece of cake in the other,
upon the merits of a certain specific for indi-
gestion, for the discovery or at least the adap-
tation of which he took credit to himself. The
subject was doubtless most interesting; but it
required a certain amount of self-control on
the part of his charming hostess to keep up
the appearance of interest and gravity with
which his lordship evidently considered that
the question ought to be discussed ; and sun-
dry side glances at Lady Adelaide might
have suggested to any one else that she was
becoming a little bored. The rest of the
party were scattered about in the vicinity
of the tea-table ; and an air of extreme snug-
ness and sociability pervaded everything.

By degrees, however, the party began to
break up. Lord Narborough, having eaten

considerably more cake than was good for him,
informed Lady Mount Easton, with an air
that was intended to be impressive, that he
had some rather important letters to write
before dinner, and feared therefore that he
must withdraw; an announcement which,
we regret to state, did not appear to produce
any great effect either upon his hostess or the
company in general. The other men gradually sneaked off, with the idea of a quiet
cigar before dressing; the ladies began to
wonder what o'clock it was, and show signs
of moving; and Gerard, who, having a rough
turn for drawing, had been for the last quarter
of an hour busily engaged upon a work of
art designed for the amusement of Lady
Mount Easton's little girl, suddenly found
himself, on looking up, alone with Lady
Adelaide, who was apparently too much
engrossed in some elaborate bead-work to
move just yet.

"Hollo, why, they're all gone!" exclaimed
Gerard; "it isn't time to dress yet, surely?"

"All, indeed!" echoed Lady Adelaide,
without looking up from her work; "you're
a nice young man to talk like that while I'm

still here. Bother these beads! I wish I was a man, and could swear at them; it would do me such a lot of good."

"Well, don't mind me," said Gerard, "swear away as much as you like, Adelaide; you may be sure I won't tell any one. Can't I help you?" and he shut up his drawing, and came over to the sofa where she was sitting, her head bent gracefully over a little table whereon lay the offending beads in question.

We have already intimated that Gerard and his *soi-disant* cousin were on very friendly terms, and that, when nothing more eligible presented itself, Lady Adelaide, who, it must be confessed, was rather more addicted to flirtation than some of her friends altogether approved of, had no objection to keeping her hand in by a little harmless practice with our hero. It had in fact come to be almost an understood thing that he should always be very devoted to her, though it was equally well understood on both sides that his devotion should never go beyond a certain point. And we are bound to admit that our friend Gerard had by no means shown himself back-

ward in taking advantage of whatever lati-
tude his fair relative might be disposed to
allow him, and that divers little cousinly
familiarities had occasionally passed between
them, especially when they were both some
years younger.

" No, you can't," she replied, "you're much
too clumsy. Your fingers are all thumbs, I
know; men's always are: besides, I don't think
I've got enough of these beastly beads to go
on with, so I shall give it up for to-night."

" Well, you're looking awfully nice, anyhow," was Gerard's somewhat inconsequent
rejoinder. " I say, Adelaide, old Ballybrack's
awfully spooney on you. How should you
like to be Lady Ballybrack? It's rather a
nice. place, isn't it? anyhow, there's lots of
hunting, as it's in the middle of the Rathmore
country, and you could ask me to come and
stay with you, you know."

" Rubbish!" was the young lady's reply;
" I'd just as soon marry you. Do you suppose I'd go and bury myself in a place like
that in order to be Mrs Cadger? No, hardly
good enough, I think. Now, get out of the
way, I'm going up to dress."

"Oh, don't go away," pleaded Gerard, lazily. "There's three quarters of an hour yet, and this sofa's so jolly comfortable."

"Well, that's more than your arm is, I can tell you. Take it away at once, sir; I won't have any nonsense. There now, you've gone and scratched yourself, you stupid boy, and serve you quite right, too. Well, what are you staring at now?"

"I was looking at that brooch of yours, Adelaide," replied Gerard, in a somewhat altered voice. "I hadn't noticed it before; where did you get it?"

"Get it?" she replied; "why, it's been in the family for ages. It belonged to Mary Queen of Scots, and there was a cross just like it, which I ought to have too; but it disappeared some time ago, mamma says, and I suppose it was stolen."

"Well, it's very odd," said Gerard, with a sigh, his thoughts wandering away from Lady Adelaide to an entirely different person; "it's very odd, but I could have sworn I had seen that cross you speak of, and that's what made me ask you. It's such a curious pattern," he continued, looking hard at the brooch,

which held together a lace arrangement of
some sort round Lady Adelaide's pretty neck,
"and the cross I saw belonged to Queen Mary
too, at least so they said—I mean I was told
so. It was a girl I met at a ball in Wealdshire, down near Sydmonton, you know,"
endeavouring to harden his voice and speak
unconcernedly, but failing signally in the
attempt, "and she had a cross just exactly
like that."

"Oh, yes, I understand," interrupted Lady
Adelaide, seeing through him in a moment,
and perhaps not particularly well pleased;
"well, you may tell your friend, with my
compliments, next time you see her, that it's
my opinion she stole it. Goodness! there's
the gong, and I've got a new dress to put on.
What a fool I've been to waste all this time
here with you!" And her ladyship was
decidedly "short" with Gerard for the rest
of that evening.

As for our hero himself, the little episode of
the brooch had set him thinking, sadly enough,
of his far-away love, and of his apparently
hopeless position as regarded her. It was
very curious, too, about that cross, which he

remembered only too well. Of course it could
not possibly be the same that Lady Adelaide
had spoken of as having been in the Narborough family ; but it certainly was odd that
there should be two crosses of that peculiar
workmanship, both of which were said to have
originally belonged to the same person. However, this was only a detail, and not worth
thinking about ; but it all recalled vividly to his
mind the events of those ten days at Shawfield,
which seemed to stand out as a landmark in
his life, and it seemed to him somehow as if
even his chronic and harmless flirtation with
Lady Adelaide, which had gone on ever since
he could remember, were a breach of faith
towards her whom he felt that he loved above
every one and everything in the world. And
yet, alas! what grounds had he for supposing
that she cared two straws about his flirting
with Lady Adelaide or any one else ? It was
all very wretched and unsatisfactory, he knew
that ; and he went to dress with rather a heavy
heart.

A good dinner, however, following on a good
day's sport, is not without its soothing effects,
even in the case of a gentleman in love ; and

the social atmosphere at Bellmoor was too cheerful to allow of any great depression of spirits. Before going to bed, therefore, Gerard felt better again, and inclined to take a more philosophical view of his prospects. He felt as if it would do him good to confide his troubles to Lady Mount Easton; but the opportunity did not present itself until the day before his departure, when, being a Sunday afternoon, and most of the other guests having departed the previous day, he had accompanied her in a walk to the house of an old retainer about a couple of miles away.

Women are very quick to find out when a man is in love, and Lady Mount Easton had not failed to notice that there was something amiss with Gerard, which she was not slow in attributing to its true cause; and being really fond of and interested in him, she felt some desire to know more about it, and had, in fact, determined to invite his confidence. So, having accomplished her visit, and proposed a slight *détour* on the road home, she approached the subject with a tact and delicacy which few knew better how to exercise.

"So glad to have had you here, Jerry," she

began, "and that you've had a little shooting. It's so fortunate, too, that you've had such fine weather ; that makes such a difference in this wild country."

" Oh, Lily," he replied, " I've enjoyed it immensely. We've really had capital sport, especially considering that it's the end of the season. But you know I always enjoy being here, apart from the shooting or anything of that sort."

"Yes, I think it seems to have done you good," she said, with a side glance at his face ; "I didn't think you were looking very well when you came, but you're looking much better now. I fancied you looked as if you had been working too hard, or perhaps," she added, in the most innocent manner possible, "as if you had had something to bother you."

This was an invitation to confidence which, coming from such a quarter, it would have required some strength of mind to resist, and which our friend was certainly not proof against. He was silent for a moment, then stammered out a few incoherent remarks as to there being nothing particular, and then came out with it all.

"Well, Lily," he said, "as you've asked me,
I don't mind telling you that I have been
rather bothered about something, and if it
won't bore you, I'll tell you all about it."
And he told her the whole story : how he had
first seen Miss Graham on the Southdowns,
but had thought no more about her till he
met her again at the Shawfield ball ; and how
he had eventually been unable to restrain himself from proposing to her. "You'll think me a
great fool, Lily, I'm sure," he continued, "but
I couldn't help it, and I'm in earnest about it,
I can tell you, if only I knew what to do."

"Dear Jerry," was the reply, "it's most
interesting to me, I assure you ; and I'm so
glad you've told me. Do you know, I fancied
there was something of this sort, for you
seemed so unlike yourself. I am sure she
must be nice, Jerry, from what you say. But
it seems to me, you know, that—well, that you
have been just a little precipitate. You say
she lives with this Mr Baldwin ; is she any
relation, or is he her guardian, or what ? "

"Well, that's just the odd part of it,"
replied Gerard, with a sigh. "It's a most extraordinary thing ; but no one seemed to know

anything about her—I mean to say, who she was ; though every one seemed to think it quite natural that she should be living there. Lady Sydmonton told me that she fancied she was the daughter of an old friend of his who was dead, and that he had adopted her as his daughter, or something of that sort. I asked two or three other people, and they said much the same thing ; but no one seemed to know for certain, and I didn't like to ask too many questions about her."

" No ; of course not," replied her ladyship, various ideas as to the relationship of the young lady to Mr Baldwin passing through her mind. " But it does seem odd, certainly, that no one should have known anything about her. Don't you think, Jerry, that perhaps it would be as well to make quite sure about her before you do anything more—I mean, exactly who she is, you know, and who her own people are ? I should think Lady Sydmonton could do that for you, couldn't she ? "

" Ah, very likely," returned Gerard ; " but then, you know, I should have to tell her all about it, and I can't talk to her as I can to you, Lily."

" Well then, Jerry, I almost think I should
wait a little, if I were you, before doing anything further.   Let me see : I wonder whether
I could find out anything about her for you.
She can't be one of the Castleton Grahams, or
I should have heard of her ; but it's a common
enough name.   I know Lady Sydmonton a
little, and I daresay I shall see her in London ;
and I might ask her myself, but," laughing,
" I am afraid she might perhaps guess my
reason for asking, and I suppose you wouldn't
care about that ? "

" Oh, Lily, it's awfully good of you, I'm
sure," replied Gerard, " but you must not
trouble yourself about it unless it comes in
your way.   The worst of it is, that when I—
when I spoke to her, you know, she seemed
so strange about it, as if there really was
some strong reason against it.   And yet she
didn't seem angry either ; and I can't help
fancying, Lily, that she rather liked me."

" Well, Jerry, I think that's quite possible,
you know.   But now, if you'll take my advice,
you won't do anything in a hurry.   It does
seem to have been a little sudden, doesn't it ?
I don't mean to suggest that you are not

thoroughly in earnest; but, you know, marriage is a serious affair, after all, and you are still very young for that sort of thing. Besides, Jerry, to speak seriously, for you know I really do take an interest in you, what sort of prospects would you have if you were to marry this young lady? You seem to live very comfortably by yourself, and I know you have got on pretty well; but I suppose your official income is not very great yet, is it? Perhaps your father would allow you something? By the way, Jerry, have you said anything to him about it yet?"

These were home-thrusts, and Gerard winced under them. "Well, Lily," he said, after a moment's hesitation, "to tell you the truth, I haven't told my father; indeed, I haven't said a word about it to any one except yourself and George Morton—you know who I mean, he's a very great friend of mine. I suppose I ought to have told my father; but somehow I didn't want to. Of course, if it had been all right, I must have told him; but, you know, he's rather odd about some things, and as it is, I thought I had better say nothing about it."

"But about the money, Jerry; you know one must think of that. What do you suppose you would have if you were to marry Miss Graham?"

"Well, Lily," he replied, "I must confess I did it rather without thinking; and, of course, when one comes to look at it seriously, it certainly does seem as if I had no business to think of such a thing. I get altogether £600 from my office, including the private secretaryship; and I fancy my father could allow me about £300 a year if he chose. He never actually told me so, but my mother has often talked to me about marrying, and she always speaks as if they would allow me something of this sort."

"Well then, Jerry, say you could produce £900 a year altogether. That's not so very bad after all, and I suppose you will get more from your office some day. Of course you don't know what Miss Graham would be likely to have? She is not an heiress, I suppose, or you would have heard of it somehow?"

"No, I don't expect she's an heiress," replied Gerard, reflectively; "she didn't at all give me the idea of that. But she might have something, Lily, you know; though, after all, I suppose I've no business to think about it."

"Well, Jerry, it seems to me that you might just have enough to begin on, perhaps; and then of course this Mr Baldwin might be able to do something. If he has no children, perhaps he may leave her his money, and she might turn out an heiress after all. Still, I really think you should wait a little, and not be in a hurry. It's a very serious thing, Jerry, as I said before; and you know you are still very young, and you might very likely do better—I mean, as regards money and all that."

"Ah, Lily," interrupted Gerard, "I only wish you could see her; I'm sure you wouldn't think I could do better in one way, at any rate."

"No, dear Jerry, I daresay not," she replied; "but still, one must think of the other too. Do you know, Jerry," with a pretty little blush, "I had rather hoped you might have taken a fancy to Helen Sartoris. She is not exactly pretty, certainly; but she's a

charming girl, and she will have £2000 a
year at least. Not that even this is so very
much now-a-days, but still there it is, and I'm
sure she would make a most charming wife for
any one."

"Dear Lily, how good of you to think about
it!" exclaimed Gerard; "I feel as if it was
quite ungrateful of me not to be in love with
Miss Sartoris; but it never occurred to me,
you know."

"Well, one could hardly expect that under
the circumstances, Jerry, and I shouldn't like
to be considered a matchmaker. However,
I am sure you had better take my advice and
not be in a hurry."

"I'll try," replied Gerard, rather mourn-
fully, "but I can't help thinking about her,
you know. But it's awfully kind of you, dear
Lily, to take such an interest in me, and I
feel ever so much better for having told you
all about it." And he took her hand, and kissed
it affectionately.

CHAPTER XXVII.

THE SAME OLD GAME.

It was the last week in March. For three weeks past a bitter east wind had desolated the face of nature, and town and country were alike unbearable. The season was unusually backward, and a sort of interregnum appeared to have set in, that was neither winter nor spring, but contrived, notwithstanding, to combine the most objectionable characteristics of both. The soft grey tints of winter had disappeared, and had given place to a monotonous drab. Here and there, in some sheltered nook, a few primroses and daffodils had ventured to show their heads, and to struggle against the inclemency of an English spring. But everything else was parched and shrivelled up. Hounds could not run over the dusty plough, the ridges of which were as hard and cutting as razors; even on the grass there was little or no scent; and one blank

day after another was beginning to convince
even the most persevering of masters that
hunting was pretty well over for that season.
In London the black dust lay thick on the
pavements, to be caught up every few minutes
by a gust of wind and whirled in the faces
and down the throats of the passers-by.   Old
and delicate people took to their beds ; and
even the young and vigorous were numbed
and petrified* by the icy blast.

Easter, however, happened to fall unusually
early this year, which made it all the more
unreasonable that the spring should be so
backward.   The House of Commons had, in
fact, reassembled after the Easter holidays,
which had been cut unusually short, with the
promise, however, that if members behaved
well and got through their work properly,
they should be allowed a longer holiday at
Whitsuntide.   London was pronounced by
some to be very full, and by others to be very
empty ; and the same difference of opinion
was expressed as to the social aspect of affairs.
Some declared that there was " nothing going
on," and that it was going to be the dullest
season on record ; while others described

themselves as already embarrassed with the number of their invitations, and prophesied a lively time for themselves and their particular friends. But whether destined to be dull or lively, the London season had once more commenced; there was already quite a respectable muster of equestrians in Rotten Row; Bond Street was full of carriages; and, surest sign of all, the various local boards and vestries, who had · been carefully watching their opportunity, had begun to pull up half the streets in the West End of London, so that locomotion was already becoming a work of the utmost difficulty and danger.

Among other persons of more or less distinction who had just arrived in the metropolis were the Dowager Lady Narborough and her daughter, who had been what the fashionable intelligence described as "sojourning" in the south of France for the last six weeks. It was Lady Adelaide's fifth season in London, and although her mother was very much attached to her, and was not haunted by any overwhelming desire to get her off her hands, she could not help feeling that it was about time that her daughter began to think

of making a suitable marriage. Not that
Lady Adelaide was by any means devoid of
admirers ; but, as we have already hinted,
she had a way of treating them which was not
always calculated to attract, and sometimes
indeed had even been known to repel. A keen
sense of humour is sometimes a dangerous gift,
especially in the case of a young lady with no
great tendency to self-restraint ; and Lady
Adelaide had more than once got into trouble
on this account, and had, in fact, in the eyes
of her more prudent elders, seriously damaged
her own prospects. For was it not perfectly
well known that the wealthy and estimable,
if slightly eccentric, Earl of Barleywater had
admired her very much during her second
season, and had, in fact, made up his mind to
propose ? And was it not equally notorious
that she had inflicted an irremediable shock
upon the feelings of that excellent young
nobleman, besides destroying her own very
good chance of becoming Countess of Barleywater, by imitating him to his face one day,
when he had come to luncheon with her and
her mamma, in a manner that even his not very
rapid powers of perception could not fail to

detect? Add to this a fondness for saying
sharp things, without always considering too
carefully the feelings of others, and it will
readily be understood that many who might
otherwise have been irresistibly attracted by
Lady Adelaide were rather shy of over-
stepping the boundary-line of mere friendship.
And yet there was nothing really ill-natured
about her. It was a wayward yet lovable
nature, impatient of restraint, but capable, in
proper hands, of being moulded into something very charming. Those who knew her
best always said that if only she came across
the right man, she would make an excellent
wife. To all appearance, however, the right
man had not yet turned up; and in the mean
time her ladyship showed no signs of any
anxiety to sacrifice her freedom.

"Well, Adelaide, what are we going to do
to-night?" inquired Lady Narborough of her
daughter, as they sat together at luncheon in
Eaton Square one drizzly, chilly day, about a
fortnight after their arrival in London. "I
suppose you won't want to drive this afternoon, and we may as well give the orders for
to-night at once."

To a casual observer, Lady Adelaide would hardly have appeared to take the amount of interest in the subject of the evening's amusement that might have been expected from a popular and fashionable young lady moving in the best set in London. She sat looking before her somewhat listlessly, and there was an air of weariness and as of something wanting about her expressive features that did not seem to indicate a mind altogether at peace with itself. Her mother's question, indeed, had to be repeated before she took any notice of it, and it appeared to be with an effort that she roused herself from her abstraction."

"Oh, I beg your pardon, mamma," she exclaimed, " I was thinking of something else. Let's see, there's Mrs Boston Smith's dance ; we must go there,—that's all, I think. There's Lady Rosemary's squash, but I don't the least want to go there, unless you think we ought to ; and then you can lie down and get a good rest after dinner, before going to Mrs Boston Smith's."

"No, my dear, I'm sure I don't want to go to Lady Rosemary's," was the reply; "and I think one thing to-night will be quite as much as is good for you. You look rather tired yourself, and I think you had better get a good rest this afternoon too."

"Oh, I'm all right, mamma, thanks," returned Lady Adelaide, carelessly. "It's only this horrid weather; it's enough to make any one look out of sorts. If it gets fine by and by, I'll take Crisp and walk over to Alice Mount Easton's to tea, and that will do me good."

"Very well, dear, only don't go and over-tire yourself."

It may possibly have been the weather that had affected Lady Adelaide's spirits, but as she sat before her looking-glass that evening, with the faithful Crisp operating upon her hair in preparation for Mrs Boston Smith's ball, it reflected an expression of pre-occupation, not to say melancholy, that would have very much astonished any of her ladyship's friends who were in the habit of seeing her only as she appeared in general society, and that could hardly have been satisfactorily accounted for by the caprices of the elements. Was it that after four years of London it had suddenly begun to dawn upon her that after all there was a good deal of vanity about the whole thing? Or had the right man appeared at last on the horizon of her life, and commenced to exercise a softening influence upon a heart that was generally supposed to be peculiarly unsusceptible to anything in the nature of a tender impression? It is possible that some speculations of this nature may have passed through the mind of Mrs Crisp as she manipulated the silky tresses into a becoming *coiffure*, with an occasional glance at the reflection of her mistress's face in the glass before her, and that, whether right or wrong, she took the liberty of forming her own conclusions on the subject. But it is not for us to pry further into the seclusion of a young lady's bedroom, and we will content ourselves with taking a glance at Lady Adelaide as she appears an hour later at Mrs Boston Smith's dance.

Mrs Boston Smith was a rich and fashionable widow, who occupied one of the largest and roomiest houses in Grosvenor Square, and whose entertainments were much sought after. The antecedents of the late lamented Mr Boston Smith had always been wrapped in obscurity, and little indeed was known as to the early history of his widow. Some said she had been a governess, and others a bar-maid; while there were not wanting those who maintained that she had been well known in certain art circles, and had in fact obtained her living as a model. Be this as it may, however, she was a clever, fascinating woman, with the remains of great beauty; and the late Boston Smith's wealth having been undisputed, whatever his means of acquiring it might have been, she had long since been taken up and pronounced the fashion by the highest authorities in London. So that a dance at the well-known corner house in the Square was pretty certain to be well patronised by the *élite* of society; and many eligible *partis* and men of distinction, social or otherwise, for whom other hostesses might angle unsuccessfully, would be found attending very regularly at Mrs Boston Smith's.

It was about half-past twelve, and the ball was in full swing. That is to say, the room "set apart" for dancing, in the language of the fashionable intelligence, was about as full as it could hold, and it might have been inferred from the character of the music that a

quadrille was being performed. But except
in a comparatively clear space at one end of
the room, where royalty was taking part in
the proceedings, the dancing was for the most
part limited to a few spasmodic advancings
and retirings, with no apparent object in
view, on the part of a few of the younger and
more energetic of the company, the majority
having evidently arrived at the conclusion
that there was too great a crowd to attempt
to go through the figures, and that it was
much more satisfactory to stand still.

In the royal set, however, the figures were
being got through with a fair amount of precision; and there was room enough for the
fresh toilettes and pretty bouquets of the per-
formers to be seen to some advantage. It
was, in fact, a very pretty sight; and as the
dancers glided backwards and forwards to the
enlivening strains of "La fille de Madame
Angot," there was enough life and anima-
tion to make up for the listless and somewhat depressing character of the proceedings
throughout the rest of the room.

In this comparatively animated circle, or,
more strictly speaking, square, might have

been observed Lady Adelaide and our old friend the "Cadger," the latter of whom had just arrived, and who, although not much addicted to dancing as a general rule, had at once solicited the honour of her ladyship's hand for this quadrille. The fact was that the "Cadger" had for some time past been very much taken with Lady Adelaide, and was as near being in love with her as was possible for a gentleman of his somewhat peculiar temperament and inclinations. "My dear fellow," he would say to a friend, taking him confidentially into a corner, "she's a d——d nice girl, I tell you; no d——d nonsense about her, and devilish clever into the bargain. I ain't a marrying man, and one has to be devilish careful, you know; but damme, if ever I were to think of that sort of thing, she's just the sort of girl that would suit me down to the ground." And so his lordship would prattle on, alternately amusing and boring his friends with his amatory confidences, but steadily increasing in devotion to Lady Adelaide, and becoming more and more convinced of her superiority to all other ladies of his acquaintance.

It was hardly to be supposed that a young lady possessed of the abilities attributed to Lady Adelaide by her admirer should not have been to some extent conscious of the sentiments she had inspired in his manly bosom ; though we are with regret compelled to state that as a rule she scarcely treated his lordship's demonstrations of affection with the consideration they deserved, and would at times, in fact, receive them with the most unbecoming levity. On the present occasion, however, she appeared less inclined to chaff him than usual, and there was an unwonted softness in her manner which was certainly very becoming to her, and which to the enamoured soul of the Earl of Ballybrack rendered her perfectly irresistible.

"I say, Lady Adelaide," observed his lordship, in the intervals of a figure, "that's an awfully nice dress you've got on. I don't understand much about ladies' dresses, you know ; but it seems to me there's something uncommon smart about yours."

"Glad you approve, Lord Ballybrack," replied her ladyship, with a pretty little curtsy. "I shall tell my maid, who makes all my things, that it has been admired by a great judge of ladies' dresses, and she will be quite pleased. Do you approve of the way she has done my hair, now, or can you suggest something different ? "

"Oh, come now ; you're chaffing, Lady Adelaide," replied the " Cadger." " But I say, do you mean to tell me your maid makes all your dresses ? By Jove, I wish I'd got a man who could make all my coats and trousers ; what a lot of trouble it would save one ! Hollo! it's my turn now." And his lordship proceeded to advance and retire with as much grace and dignity as the highly-polished floor would admit of.

"No end of a crowd here to-night," he observed, by way of an original remark, on his return to his partner, "and there'll be some more fellows up from the House soon. I saw Ravendale and some other chaps at the Carlton before dinner, and they said they meant to look in here if they could. Ah! there's Ravendale in the doorway now. Thanks, Lady Adelaide," as the music abruptly stopped, "will you come and have some tea ? it's awfully hot in here."

"Thanks very much, Lord Ballybrack, but I think I'll stop here with mamma. There she is in the corner, by the window. Another dance? oh, I really can't say now ; you must come back by and by."

It might possibly have occurred to a very close observer that Lady Adelaide's manner, which up to the present moment had had the effect of putting the "Cadger" very much at his ease, and had rendered her even more than usually charming in that enamoured nobleman's eyes, had suddenly undergone a change, and that, from having been affable in the extreme, and apparently quite disposed to encourage his lordship's not very intellectual conversation, she now manifested a somewhat unaccountable anxiety to get rid of him. Whether the "Cadger's" reference to Lord Ravendale, and the almost simultaneous appearance of that statesman, could have had anything to do with the matter it would be out of place to inquire ; but there was no doubt that, as he caught her eye, and made his way through the crowd to where she was standing, a slight though very becoming blush might have been observed to steal over her ladyship's face, and that her expression lighted up in a manner that it certainly had not done during her conversation with the " Cadger." And yet, whether owing to the proverbial inconsistency of the female mind, or to some other cause beyond our divination, her reception of the Vice-President was not marked by any unusual demonstration of cordiality, and it would have required a very penetrating and experienced observer to construct any matrimonial hypothesis out of their meeting.

" How d'ye do, Lady Adelaide ? " said his lordship, as he reached her corner ; " how are you getting on ? I've only just come up from the House, but there seem to be lots of people here."

" Yes, it's rather too much of a crowd just now, isn't it ? but it will get better by and by. What have you been doing at the House, Lord Ravendale ? Usual old story, I suppose ? "

" Oh yes," replied his lordship, " I've been hanging about there, doing nothing whatever really. We thought we should get into Supply, and I'd got some votes to look after, but there's no chance of it to-night now, so I came

away for a look in here, which seems much
more amusing. Are you going to dance this
valse, Lady Adelaide?" as the music again
struck up; "if not, come and have some supper.
The supper-room is open, for I looked in as I
came upstairs."

"Very well," replied Lady Adelaide, "I've
a sort of idea that I'm engaged for this dance,
but I don't mind chancing it; only we must
go at once," she added, with a laugh, "or my
young man will be after me." And placing
her pretty hand on Lord Ravendale's arm, they
slipped out by a side door, and joined the string
of supper-seekers on the stairs.

"How well Lady Adelaide looks to-night!"
observed that consummate judge of beauty,
little Billy Treadcroft of the Blues, as he stood
with 'a knot of non-dancing men about the
entrance to a temporary structure off the ball-
room, lighted with Chinese lanterns of various
patterns, and carefully arranged with a view
to the comfort of those who might desire
seclusion. "Look at her there, on the sofa
with Ravendale. By Jove! I wonder whether
he means business!"

"Lord bless you, no!" responded another

of the group. " Ravendale ain't a marrying man. Yes, she does look devilish well to-night, but, mind you, I ain't sure that she wouldn't be a rum 'un to marry. However, that don't matter to you or me, Billy, my boy. Come along and have some supper."

"Well, she must have enjoyed her ball," thought the worthy though sleepy Mrs Crisp, as she brushed out her mistress's silky hair that night, or rather in the small hours of the morning, "for she looks ever so much better than before she started. I wish she'd marry now, and have done with it; she'd be ever so much happier, and perhaps I shouldn't have to sit up so much at night waiting for her. There's three o'clock striking! Good-night, my lady."

CHAPTER XXVIII.

UNCERTAINTY.

THOSE who are familiar with the network of small streets that occupies the space between Pall Mall and Piccadilly, will probably have noticed, at some period of their lives, a somewhat peculiar building at the corner of a certain quiet little street not above a couple of hundred yards away from St. James's Square. The edifice in question has certainly no pretensions to architectural beauty, the exterior, as seen from the street, being suggestive of something between a riding-school and a railway station. The occupants appear to be unfamiliar with the use of windows, and the only means of ingress, consisting of a swing-door at the top of a little flight of steps, adorned with the legend "Private," presents the commonplace and prosaic appearance of the entrance to a warehouse or office. The amount of business, however, transacted on the premises would not appear to be very great, for, up till four or five o'clock in the afternoon, not a living creature will be observed to go in or out. But about five o'clock some signs of life will begin to manifest themselves. First, one or two elderly but smart-looking gentlemen will be observed to ascend the steps and pass through the swing-door ; then three or four more, younger men perhaps, in quick succession ; and so on, till by half-past six, from fifteen to twenty-five individuals of all ages from eighteen to sixty, including probably one or two guardsmen in uniform, will have entered the building. At about seven o'clock there will be a rapid exodus, the out-comers presenting the comfortable and self-satisfied appearance that may be observed on the countenances of gentlemen who have just emerged from a Turkish bath, or who have been engaged in some strong exercise for which they feel all the better ; and by half-past seven the building will be once more silent and deserted.

Without indulging in any further mystery, we may as well inform those of our readers to whom the above description does not convey

any particular significance, that the edifice
in question is the home of the London School
of Arms, an institution much patronised by a
select circle of guardsmen, Government officials,
and gentlemen at large, who are devotees of
the ancient and, fascinating science of fencing, or who delight themselves in gymnastics
and feats of strength and agility. Should a
stranger be passing by at the moment when
any one is going in or out, he will hear through
the door strange sounds of stamping, bumping,
and words of command in a foreign tongue.
And should his curiosity lead him to mount
the steps, and, regardless of the warning as to
privacy, peep in through the door, he would
find himself in a spacious and lofty apartment,
some seventy feet long by thirty wide, lighted
from the roof by a long skylight, the walls hung
round with rows of foils, masks, broadswords,
etc., and the open space in the centre occupied
by couples engaged in fencing. Round the
room may be seen parallel bars, trapézes, and
gymnastic appliances of every description;
and a staircase at either end leads to a gallery
of dressing-rooms supplied with baths and
other comforts of a private club.

It would be difficult to over-estimate the benefits offered by an institution of this kind to any person, of naturally active habits, who is compelled by circumstances to lead a comparatively sedentary life. An hour's exercise under a gymnastic instructor or with the foils has a wonderful effect in counteracting the depressing and weakening influence of a day passed in office work ; or, as was expressed by George Morton, himself an old member of the club, in forcible, if homely language, when introducing his friend Gerard, " You can be all day at that rotten old shop of yours, come here and get a real good sweat, and then have a bath, and go out to dinner, feeling almost as fit as if you had had a day's hunting."

Our friend Gerard had been by no means slow to recognise the advantages thus graphically pointed out to him ; and, at the period of our story, had not only been for some time a pretty constant *habitué* of the place, but had become a fair adept in the art of fencing, to say nothing of boxing, single-stick, and other miscellaneous exercises. It was a special resource to him during the parliamentary season, when he was kept close at his work, and could seldom get away for a day's cricket or other outdoor amusement; and having passed the whole day in the not very invigorating atmosphere of the General Enquiry Office, he would drop in at the School of Arms for an hour on his way home, and emerge, as correctly put by his friend Morton, feeling very much the better for it, and quite ready to enjoy his dinner. And since he had arrived at the position of a man in love, he had resorted to the institution more than ever, finding in it the means not only of healthy exercise, but of escaping for the time from the burden of his own thoughts. There are few things that require a more entire concentration of the faculties, both mental and physical, than the practice either of fencing or boxing; and it would indeed be difficult to think of anything else when you have once crossed blades with your adversary, and are watching every movement of eye and hand for an opening lunge, or when you are engaged in manœuvring to plant a successful hit upon your opponent's nose, and at the same time protect your own from a like assault.

One evening, then, about the beginning of May, Gerard, who had been working hard at his office all day, passed through the swing-door of the London School of Arms about half-past six, with the view of getting half an hour's exercise before dining with the Mount Eastons, from whom he had received an invitation an hour or two before, his presence being desired to fill up a sudden gap in the party. He was late, and was making the best of his way upstairs to change his clothes, when he was stopped by M. Pierre, the principal *maitre-d'armes* of the establishment, who, foil in hand, called after him with the air of a person who had some communication to make.

"Ah, Monsieur Courtenay, vous arrivez trop tard," he observed, "voilà M. Morton qui vient de vous demander."

"M. Morton!" exclaimed Gerard, pausing on the stairs, "c'est impossible; il est parti—il est à la campagne. By Jove," he thought, half reproaching himself for not having thought much about his friend lately, "surely he can't be back again, or he would have let me know."

" Non, non, c'était bien M. Morton," repeated M. Pierre, " voilà plus de six mois que
je l'ai vu, mais il est venu ce soir, et il vous
demandait. Un autre monsieur est venu avec
lui—un vieillard, et par exemple il à laissé
son parapluie," pointing to an umbrella in a
corner. " Mais depêchez-vous, mettez votre
veste, et venez prendre votre leçon."

" Well, he must have been here," thought
Gerard, as he went upstairs, " but I wonder
he didn't tell me. I must go and look him
up. Poor old George, I wonder how he's
getting on ! There's something precious odd
about the whole business."

Although, as we have already mentioned,
there was a plentiful supply of private dressing-rooms for the use of the members of
the London School of Arms, it was found in
practice that the majority preferred sociability
to privacy, and were wont to avail themselves of a large public room, where they
could indulge freely in conversation while
dressing or undressing, and could in cold
weather enjoy the advantage of a good fire.
This apartment was presided over by the
principal custodian of the club, an official of

long standing and profound respectability, who, had it not been for an imperturbably courteous and obliging manner, and the gift of being everywhere at once, might at times, when the room was crowded, have found his position rather a trying one ; for being summoned or appealed to every moment, it was about as much as he could do to respond to the many demands upon his attention. "Towel please, Jones!" " I say, Jones, there's no hot water to-night!" " Jones, just ask Lord Lollypop not to sit on my hat." " Hollo, Jones! sorry to see your name in the police court again this morning!" "Look here, Jones ; here's Captain Overalls taken my umbrella, and left that beastly old sword of his instead!" Amid all which badinage Mr Jones, preserving, according to his wont, a perfectly unruffled demeanour, glided hither and thither in the active discharge of his duties, neglecting no one, and attending to each individual requirement with a precision that was truly marvellous. Meanwhile, from the hall or *salle d'armes* below an incessant Babel of sounds ascended to the upper region. " Fondez-vous!" " Carte, contre-carte et riposte!"

from the French professors. "One, two,
straighten the arms; slowly down to the
sides!" from the gymnastic instructor;
mingled with the clash of foils, the bumping
of dumb-bells, and the various other noises
incidental to the pursuits to which the establishment was consecrated.

Gerard lost no time in changing his clothes;
and in another five minutes had descended to
the lower floor, clad in flannels and fencing-
jacket. Just at this moment he caught sight
of M. Pierre in conversation with some one at
the door, for whom he was holding it open.
But before Gerard had got half across the
room, the door was shut, and the stranger,
whoever he was, had disappeared.

"Ah, mais voilà monsieur qui revient!"
exclaimed Pierre, as he caught sight of
Gerard. "Il est rentré chercher son parapluie,
mais il était bien pressé, et il ne pouvait
rester. C'est bien dommage que vous n'étiez
pas ici; peut-être vous aurait-il donné des
nouvelles de M. Morton."

"Oh, c'est égal," replied Gerard, unconcernedly, "M. Morton reviendra sans doute
dans quelques jours." But he felt annoyed,

all the same, at having missed the chance of
hearing something of George, especially as he
was unable to avoid a twinge or two of con-
science for having of late been so absorbed in
his own affairs as to have almost forgotten his
friend. For, during the last fortnight or so,
Gerard's peace of mind had been greatly
disturbed. It would be doing him an in-
justice to say that he had at any time forgotten his lady-love ; but, at the same time,
the distraction of his official work and the
bustle of London life had served to divert his
thoughts in a great measure from the one
all-absorbing topic that had for some time
occupied them. All of a sudden, however, an
event had occurred which had thrown him
back into much the same state of mind that
he had been in four or five months before. In
other words, he had seen Florence in London.
Not indeed, to speak to, which would have
altogether finished him, but he had caught a
glimpse of her in a brougham in Piccadilly,
in company with an elderly lady of, as
it appeared to him, a somewhat stern and
forbidding aspect, whom he at once set down
as ill-disposed towards himself and likely to

injure whatever prospects he might have with
Florence.   And she had seen him too; and he
hardly knew whether he had been made more
happy or more miserable by the look that
came into her face as she half involuntarily
bent forward and her eyes met his.   He stood
looking after the carriage as if in a dream, till
it had disappeared out of sight, and then
began almost unconsciously to walk rapidly in
the direction it had taken.   A few moments,
however, brought him to his senses, and convinced him of the hopelessness of such a
pursuit; and then he began to blame himself
for not having followed the carriage at once.
Was it possible that he had actually seen her
again!   And that look in her eyes; surely
she must care for him after all, or she could
never have looked like that; and yet, perhaps
after all it was only his fancy.   Then he tried
to remember how she was dressed, and was
furious with himself for having only noticed
that she wore a light-coloured dress, while he
could not remember whether she had on a hat
or a bonnet, though his impression rather
inclined to the former.   Occupied with such
reflections, he turned mechanically down Duke

Street, and wandered on in a vague, aimless sort of way, till he found himself at the steps leading down from the Duke of York's monument into St. James's Park. It was about three o'clock in the afternoon; his chief, who had been down at Newmarket, was not expected till four, and he had nothing particular to do for the next half-hour. He went into the park, and sat down on a chair near the water. It was a lovely spring day. All around, the tender foliage, as yet unsullied by London smoke, was bursting into life. The flower-beds were bright with tulips; a blackbird was singing merrily from an adjoining thicket, and the air was fresh with the scent of new-mown grass. The wild-fowl were quacking and diving merrily in mid-stream, or congregated round certain spots where bands of juveniles were engaged in casting on the waters the accumulations of the nursery breadbasket. Everything wore a look of life and brightness, and even the dingy and soot-encumbered buildings in the background were warmed up into a not unpleasing mass of colour by the genial rays of the sun. But to Gerard everything for the moment seemed blank and dreary. He had seen his love again, and though he felt that he loved her more passionately than ever, it seemed to him as if the gulf between them were deeper and deeper. There she was in London, probably within a mile of him at that very moment, and yet he was as effectually separated from her as if the Atlantic rolled between them. Somehow or other, the possibility of meeting her again under existing circumstances had never occurred to him. It seemed to him as if that never-to-be-forgotten parting in the library at Crowhurst had placed an insurmountable barrier between them, insurmountable at least until the mystery which seemed to hang about her should be cleared up. For a mystery there was beyond doubt; otherwise, how could he account for the tone of distress, almost of misery, in which she had spoken of herself? And yet, what could he do? for he had no possible means of unravelling her history, and he instinctively shrank from anything that might appear like intruding himself upon her. For, to do him justice, he was by no means blind to the fact that, from a worldly and practical point of view, his prospects as regarded Miss Graham, even supposing other influences to be favourable, could not be considered as otherwise than extremely problematical. He was obliged to confess to himself that he had made a proposal of marriage without any ostensible means of entering upon that highly honourable state, and that if he were called upon to explain how he proposed to maintain Miss Graham in the position to which she had previously been accustomed, he might appear rather at a disadvantage. He felt, in fact, that his proposal had been most rash and ill-considered, and that he had no right whatever, under existing circumstances, to press his suit any further.

It will readily be understood, therefore, that Gerard's reflections that bright May afternoon were far from being in keeping with the surroundings; and during the rest of that day, and the next two or three days, he had very nearly reverted to his original state of hopelessness and despondency. Here again, however, the precious solace and distraction of hard work came to his aid; and it being the

height of the session, and business at the
General Enquiry Office in consequence pretty
lively, he had happily but little leisure for
indulging in the contemplation of his own
affairs.

CHAPTER XXIX.

"WHO IS SHE?"

HAD Gerard by any means succeeded in following up the carriage which held all that for the time being was dearest to him in the world, he would have found himself at the door of what would be described in an auctioneer's or house-agent's advertisement as a substantial family mansion in Portland Place—not one of the very largest houses in that highly respectable locality, but presenting at the same time every appearance of comfort if not of affluence. The door was opened, before the footman had time to descend and ring the bell, by a grey-headed old gentleman out of livery, whose appearance was quite in keeping with the exterior of the house, and who bustled out to assist the occupants of the carriage to alight. The first to appear was the elderly lady whom Gerard had noticed, and who, to any disinterested observer, would have seemed the embodiment of all that was harmless and inoffensive. She was followed by Miss Graham, who, in her pretty morning-dress of some light summer material, would certainly have appeared none the less attractive to Gerard than in her riding-habit, in which costume he had been more accustomed to see her during that brief period of happiness which seemed to him to have passed away for ever.

"Gregson, I shall not want the carriage again till a quarter to eight, and I shall be at home to any one who calls after five. Florence dear, you look tired; you had better go and rest yourself till tea-time, and I will send Edwards to you with some sal-volatile."

"Thanks, so much, dear Mrs Ashton," was the reply; "I think I will go and rest for a little if you don't mind, as I've got rather a headache. I think perhaps it is the sudden heat, but I shall be all right by and by."

"Yes, dear, go and lie down, that will be the best thing for you. Gregson, send Edwards to my room, and then come to the drawing-room; I have got a note to send. Never mind me, Florence dear, you go and lie down at once."

As we have no desire to indulge in unneces-
sary mystery, we may as well inform our
readers at once that the estimable lady whom
we have just introduced to them, and under
whose hospitable roof Florence was for the
time domiciled, was Mr Baldwin's only sister,
who had been for some years a widow, and
who, being of a kind-hearted and benevolent
disposition, and having no children of her
own, had for some time past adopted Florence
as a sort of niece, and was always glad to
have her as an inmate of the roomy and
comfortable house in Portland Place. And
though Florence infinitely preferred Netherdean to London, and was more at home
on the Southdowns than in Hyde Park or
Bond Street, she was much attached to the
old lady, who had taken a great fancy to
her, and done her many little kindnesses;
and the result was that she was generally
to be found two or three times a year on a
visit to Mrs Ashton.

As is usually the case in such establishments, Mrs Ashton was tyrannised over by a
select circle of old family servants, who had all
waxed fat and sleek in her service, and whose

great object seemed to be to combine the maximum of good living with the minimum of work. At the same time, they were all more or less attached to her, and would gladly have done anything to serve her that did not materially interfere with their own comfort and convenience. A fair share of this good feeling was extended to Florence, especially on the part of Mr Gregson the butler, who, having been pleased to propound the theory that she was delicate and required " keeping up," was much given to pressing upon her at luncheon-time some rare old sherry of his mistress', with the restorative qualities of which it was generally supposed that he himself was practically acquainted; and he had recently even gone so far as to express to Mrs Ashton his opinion that Miss Florence was not looking strong, and that a couple of glasses of wine at luncheon and the same allowance at dinner would be a more effective form of tonic than any amount of doctors' prescriptions. The general verdict, in fact, both of housekeeper's room and servants' hall, was that Miss Florence was a nice young lady who gave no trouble, and to whom therefore they had no objection as an occasional inmate of their establishment.

“ Well, Edwards,” inquired Mrs Ashton, awaking from a nap as that confidential domestic softly entered her room to inform her that tea was ready in the drawing-room, “ how is Miss Florence ? did you give her some sal-volatile ? ”

“ Yes, ma'm, I took it up to Miss Florence's room, but she said she wouldn't have it just then, and asked me to leave it. She didn't seem very well, though, ma'm, and she looked to me as if—as if she'd been a-crying.”

“ Crying ! nonsense, Edwards,” returned Mrs Ashton, indignantly. “ Why, what should she be crying about ? ”

“ I don't know, I'm sure, ma'm ; but she turned her head away when I went in, and her voice didn't seem quite natural, somehow.”

“ Ah, she had a headache, poor child, and wasn't feeling well,” replied Mrs Ashton ; “ she certainly doesn't seem very strong just now. She's a nice child, Florence,” she went on, half to herself ; “ what a sad thing it is ”—— And then she suddenly stopped, re-collecting that Edwards was present, and that it might not be altogether desirable to take her too much into her confidence.

It is hardly necessary to observe that Miss Graham's position in Mr Baldwin's household had for some time been a subject of much speculation and gossip, not only among the other members of his establishment, but also among those of his sister's, the two families being on intimate terms, and the affairs of their respective master and mistress forming a common topic for discussion. It was agreed on all sides that there was something very mysterious about the whole affair. All that was known of her advent into the family was that, some years before, Mr Baldwin had left home rather suddenly, had been absent, no one knew where, for about a fortnight, and had returned home one fine September evening, accompanied by a girl of about thirteen, and a ladylike person who appeared to be in the position of a governess. No announcement had been made of this addition to the family, beyond a letter received that morning from Mr Baldwin by Mrs Styles, the housekeeper, requesting that two specified rooms, opening into each other, might be got ready for immediate occupation. Mr Baldwin, although a man of simple tastes and habits, and accustomed to be a good deal tyrannised over by his household in minor matters, was nevertheless not a man to be disobeyed or slighted with impunity when he had once given an order; and although Mrs Styles' curiosity was excited to a very high pitch by the intimation she had received, she at once set to work to carry out her master's directions.

By half-past six in the evening, the time when Mr Baldwin and his visitors might be expected, the excitement of the household had been wound up to fever heat; and when, after much waiting and listening, the long-expected wheels of the Shawfield fly were heard grinding up the road and turning into the approach, there was scarcely a window or other coign of vantage commanding a view of the front door that was not occupied by an eager spectator, watching anxiously for a glimpse of the new arrivals. Out got Mr Baldwin in his usual deliberate way, and calmly proceeded to hand out first a lady dressed in black, with a thick veil over her face, and then a slight, graceful girl in a short frock, who gazed about her with a half-

frightened, half-curious look in her soft brown
eyes.   Leading the way into the house, he presented the new comer to the curtsying and
officious Mrs Styles, with an intimation that
they had had a long journey, and would be
glad to go to their rooms.   They did not
appear again that evening, some supper being
taken up to them by Mr Baldwin's desire ; and
all that the expectant household were able to
glean from Mrs Styles, whose natural self-import-
ance was materially increased by having been
to a certain extent taken into confidence in
the matter, was that the elder lady's name was
Mrs Caledon, and that of the younger Miss
Florence Graham.

Without going into further details, it will
be sufficient to state that from this evening
Mrs Caledon and Miss Graham became permanent members of Mr Baldwin's establishment, and that as the household became
accustomed to their presence, the interest
which their sudden advent had created
gradually died away.   It soon appeared that
Mrs Caledon was in charge of Mrs Graham's
education, and a set of rooms were assigned
to their special use.   It was understood, not

exactly on Mr Baldwin's authority, but without direct contradiction on his part, that Miss Graham was the orphan child of an old friend of his who had died abroad, and that it was his intention to adopt and bring her up as his own. This alone had a pleasant flavour of mystery about it, and many and various were the speculations regarding the deceased friend who had left such an interesting charge to Mr Baldwin. We regret, indeed, to be obliged to confess that the character of that estimable gentleman did not pass altogether scatheless at the hands of the gossips of Netherdean and the neighbourhood. Not only did his lady-friends ask each other, in the most innocent manner, whether Miss Graham was at all like him, and whether he seemed much attached to her or not, but frequent and more meaning remarks were indulged in respecting the lady who had accompanied her. " Who *is* this Mrs Caledon ? " " Is she a lady, or only a governess ? " " Is it really true that she sits at the head of the table, and does the honours for Mr Baldwin ? " " Really, my dear, I think one ought to know something more about it. Mr Baldwin is very eccentric, of

course, and not exactly in our society, you
know; but still, one doesn't like to have
this sort of thing going on under one's
very eyes, as it were." And so on, in the
usual charitable strain so common among a
certain class of women, who, kind as they
may be, and very likely are at heart, are
seldom able to resist the temptation of a
sly hit at the reputation of one of their
own sex.

But neither Mr Baldwin, Mrs Caledon, nor
little Florence were much affected by the
suspicions or innuendoes of their neighbours.
The former gentleman pursued his studies as
usual, and took his walks or rides about
Netherdean with the most serene indifference
to and apparent unconsciousness of what
might be whispered abroad as to his domestic
arrangements. Mrs Caledon, on her part, had
been but a very short time an inmate of
Netherdean before it became apparent to the
establishment in general, and in fact to every
one who had anything to do with her, that
she was not a person to be treated with anything but the most profound respect. It is
true that having, at Mr Baldwin's request,

assumed the head of the table when they were
alone, she did not vacate that position on the
rare occasions when any one else was present ;
but in other respects it would have required
an imaginative genius or a peculiarly slander-
ous tongue to have set on foot or maintained
anything in the nature of a scandal. Not that
the elementary materials for the construction
of a malicious story were altogether wanting,
if the fact of a handsome young woman having
come, under somewhat peculiar circumstances,
to reside in the house of an elderly bachelor,
himself a man whose life had always been
surrounded by a certain degree of mystery,
could be held to afford such. For handsome
Mrs Caledon undeniably was, and apparently
quite young enough to have excited the
curiosity, if not the jealousy, of the fair sex
in the neighbourhood of Netherdean. But, so
far from being desirous to attract attention,
her great object appeared to be to discourage
it ; and more than one enterprising gentleman,
who were curious to see "what old Baldwin
had got hold of," and had on various pretexts
effected an entrance to Netherdean in the con-
fident expectation of making an impression on

the handsome governess, were compelled to
retire ignominiously under the chilling reception accorded them, and to confess that " by
Jove, you know, she won't stand any nonsense. Something about her makes you feel
precious awkward. Not business, eh? must
be a man somewhere in the background,—
can't possibly be old Baldwin." Such, at least,
were the covertly expressed sentiments of
those adventurous youths who had in vain
tried their fascinations upon her, and had
come to the mortifying conclusion that all
efforts in that direction were unavailing.

As for little Florence, her childish life was
altogether undisturbed by the speculations
and comments to which her appearance at
Netherdean had given rise. Of a shy and
timid disposition, it had been some time
before she had become accustomed to her
new home and the strange faces around her.
But by degrees the new life became more
and more attractive, and by the end of a
year she seemed a different creature. The
pure, sweet air of the Southdowns seemed
to agree with her wonderfully, and under
the gentle and affectionate discipline of Mrs

Caledon her life was certainly far from being
an unhappy one. The pretty, graceful child
soon became a favourite with every one about
the place; though it must be confessed that,
next to Mrs Caledon, her affections were
principally centred upon Peter, the old coachman who has already been introduced to our
readers, and to whom was intrusted the congenial task of teaching her to ride. And an
apt pupil she proved, as the old man would
tell the neighbours with pride; and it was
not long before she was promoted from her
first mount, a sedate old pony that had been
about the place for years, to an animal of
improved paces and more lively temperament.
It was a pretty sight to see the pair careering
over the downs together on a fine summer's
morning,—old Peter on a big brown horse,
that had been a good hunter in his day, in
his dark-grey cut-away coat and neat drab
breeches and gaiters, his weather-beaten face
lit up with a proud smile as he kept a watch-
ful eye on the sweet girlish figure by his side,
swaying easily to every motion of her spirited
little pony, sitting well back, hands well down,
and her soft brown hair streaming in the

wind.   The girl, in fact, took as naturally to
riding as a duck to water; and by the time
she was seventeen it would have been difficult to find any one of her own years and
experience who had either a better seat or
better hands on a horse than Florence Graham.
It was, perhaps, the happiest moment of her
life when, about this period, she became the
possessor of " Kathleen," and, to her unspeak-
able delight, was allowed to go out occasionally with the harriers.   With her first day's
fox - hunting and its results the reader is
already familiar.

Florence's life at Netherdean, then, though
perhaps somewhat lonely, had been by no
means an unhappy one.   It was some little
time before she became accustomed to Mr
Baldwin, whose dry formal manner and pre-
cise old bachelor habits were not, perhaps,
best calculated to win the affections of a young
girl.   But no one could be long in his company without finding out that beneath a somewhat unprepossessing exterior there lurked a
gentleness of disposition and a kindliness of
heart that it would have been impossible not
to appreciate.   Florence had not been a year

at Netherdean before she and Mr Baldwin
were firm friends; and by the time she had
reached sixteen, that charming borderland
between childhood and womanhood which, in
some respects, is more fascinating than any
other age, she could twist her "padre," as he
had been playfully styled one day by his friend
Mr Montenello, from a supposed resemblance
to some South American ecclesiastic, round
her little finger. Mrs Caledon, it should be
observed, had relinquished her charge soon
after her sixteenth birthday, and though
Florence felt the loss of her friend and governess very keenly, she had no particular fancy
for another domestic preceptress, and had by
this time sufficient influence over Mr Baldwin
to persuade him that it would be quite sufficient for the completion of her education—far
better for her, in fact, in every respect—if she
were to take advantage of Mrs Ashton's kindness, and have some finishing lessons from
various masters during her regular and generally somewhat protracted visits to Portland
Place.

At sixteen, therefore, Florence found herself,

to all intents and purposes, in the position of mistress of Netherdean. Not that this position had been in any way sought by her, or that it would ever have occurred to her to take advantage of it. Mr Baldwin, as we have already observed, although mild and tractable to the last degree, was a man who liked to be master in his own house, and would, in his own quiet way, have speedily suppressed anything in the shape of an usurpation of his authority. But he had learned to love and cherish the graceful girl who had now for some years been the brightness of his formerly lonely and solitary home, and he would miss her sadly when the time came round for one of her periodical visits to his sister. On her part, Florence had become almost as much attached to the old man as he was to her; and though, with the waywardness of her sex, she would occasionally take a mischievous delight in a little teasing, her fits of " contrariness " never lasted long; and on the whole, no father and daughter could have been more united than this outwardly incongruous pair. There was one subject, indeed, which was to Florence a perpetual and increasing sorrow, and which was the only cloud over her otherwise happy life. And this, by the way, brings us back to the point whence we started at the commencement of this chapter.

CHAPTER XXX.

EASTHAMPTON PARK.

AUTUMN once more—that sweetly melancholy period of the year, when we suddenly begin to realise that there are but three or four months left before the time when another Christmas will be upon us, and another year will have been added to the past; a period closely allied in many respects to the autumn of life, to that vague state when one man will be described as middle-aged and another as elderly, but where, in any case, it has become evident that the summer of life is irrevocably gone, and that, although the autumn may be very beautiful and very enjoyable, the next stage must surely be winter, and after that there can be no great change until the very last.

But while it lasts, there can be no doubt that autumn is very pleasant, and is to many persons the most enjoyable and most eagerly anticipated season of the year. For not only is

it synonymous with the opening of the shooting and hunting season, and with the commencement of the pleasantest period of country-house life, but to hundreds and thousands
of busy workers, whose position debars them
from a participation in the sports of the field,
or whose inclinations lead them in other directions, the approach of autumn implies a short
relaxation from the drudgery of daily life, and
the exchange of the used-up atmosphere of
London for the invigorating breezes of the
country or sea-side. Autumn brings with it,
in fact, a sense of rest and placid enjoyment
that belongs to no other season of the year;
and its peculiar attributes have many a
counterpart in the corresponding period of
human life. It has been truly said by one of
the most observant and sympathetic of modern
novelists that a really beautiful woman is
never so attractive as when her loveliness
is slightly on the wane ; and as for the
pleasures and advantages of male fogeydom,
there are not wanting those who maintain
that they may be favourably compared with
the feverish aspirations of early youth.

But whichever way we look at it, the year

will pass away, and however long the golden
brightness of the summer may linger with us,
it will surely be succeeded by the sober calm
of autumn. And once more the autumn had
arrived for Gerard Courtenay, who, looking
back to the corresponding period of the previous year, could hardly believe that it was
nearly twelve months since that memorable
night of the Shawfield ball, which had so
changed the whole aspect of his life. The
summer had slipped by with him very quickly;
and with the exception of that single glimpse of
Florence in the street, there had been nothing
remarkable to disturb the quiet tenor of his
life. Work, that blessed distraction of a
troubled spirit, had kept him from thinking
too much about himself. The session had
been an unusually heavy one, and the multi-
farious duties of the Vice-President of the
General Enquiry Office had seldom called for
closer attention. Gerard had indeed for the
first time begun to take a real interest in his
work and a strong personal attachment to
his chief, who on his part had settled down to
the routine life of a Minister in a manner that
was a source of unceasing astonishment to

most of his old friends and acquaintances—
had had the effect of making him throw himself into it heart and soul. And the more he
devoted himself to his work, the less he seemed
to care for the old business of the London
season, the ceaseless repetition of balls and
parties, and the usual "knocking about."
Everything seemed changed in this respect
to him since last year; he now experienced
a sort of shyness in going into a ball-room,
and a feeling as if every one knew that he
had proposed to a girl, and had been rejected;
and although this uncomfortable sensation
would generally wear off after a time, and he
would sometimes enjoy a ball almost as much
as ever, it was not quite the same thing.
And so he gradually began to drop out of the
ruck of ball-going young men; and although
a certain number of cards continued to be left
at his lodgings or at the office, it was seldom
that he would take advantage of them, and
was more often to be found under the gallery
of the House of Commons, to which, as private
secretary to a Minister, he had by courtesy
the *entrée*, than in the "gilded saloons"
of the fashionable world. In short, our

friend seemed in a very fair way to become a
highly respectable and hard-working member
of society.

It must not be supposed, however, that
the blighted state of his affections had altogether deprived him of the power of enjoying
life. He had gone in more than ever for such
out-door sports and exercises as were open to
him, and was beginning to be noticed by the
veteran swordsmen of the London School of
Arms as one of the most promising of the
younger division. He was still, moreover,
the possessor of the two noble animals which
had carried him through the previous hunting
season, and was beginning to look forward to
another with a keenness which surprised himself. He had not unnaturally begun to
connect his lady-love with his happiest recollections of the hunting-field ; and without
actually going so far as to contemplate
another visit to the Underdown country, he
had a sort of vague idea that another hunting
season might in some way or other bring them
together again. So far, he had stuck stead-
fastly to his resolution not to attempt to see
her again for the present, in which act of self-

abnegation he had been encouraged to the
utmost by Lady Mount Easton, who, having
originally made him promise to take no
further action in the matter for six months,
had subsequently urged him to leave it alone
till the end of the year. "If by that time,
Jerry," she said, "you feel really and truly
the same about her, why then I won't say
anything more, and, depend upon it, you
won't lose anything by waiting. If she
really cares about you at all, it's not likely
she will have married any one else by that
time; and perhaps your own prospects may
have improved; for you know, dear Jerry,"
she added, "you won't mind my saying so,
but unless she turns out to be an heiress, you
really won't have much to marry upon." And
such was Gerard's devotion to and belief in
his charming cousin, that although he himself
had no doubt whatever as to the strength
of his attachment, and it was a hard struggle
to give up all idea of even seeing Florence
until another winter should come round, by
which time all sorts of complications and
difficulties might have arisen, he adopted her
advice with the most exemplary fortitude,

and endeavoured, though with indifferent success, to think as little about Netherdean and its fair occupant as possible.

As the months rolled on, however, he began to feel that the time was approaching when he could bear his state of uncertainty and suspense no longer, and that, come what might, he must see Florence once more. In the meantime he had a week or two at his disposal, and having been detained in or about London during the greater part of September, he was now, at the end of the first week of October, looking forward to some rough occasional shooting at Easthampton Park, the ancestral seat of his quasi-relative, the Earl of Narborough.

It will be apparent to our readers, from what we have already said of this nobleman's character or proclivities, that he was not violently addicted to field - sports of any description. But, being the possessor of a property which contained in itself what an auctioneer or estate agent would describe as exceptional natural advantages for the rearing and preservation of game, he felt constrained to keep up a certain amount of shooting, and although, despite the entreaties and representations of his keeper, he did next to nothing in the way of rearing pheasants, the warm, sheltered dells and copses with which the higher ground about the park was intersected, were always tenanted by a fair show of wild birds; while the low-lying ground towards the estuary which skirted one side of the property for several miles afforded very respectable partridge-shooting. So that, on the whole, there was better sport to be obtained on his lordship's comparatively unpreserved property than on many others less favoured by nature, where large sums were annually expended on the artificial production of game.

Easthampton Park was situated at the south-western extremity of Wealdshire; but although in the same county as Sydmonton and other localities we have already described, it was in a different sort of country altogether. The downs here take a bend inland, and the high ground gradually slopes down to a flat, low-lying seaboard, intersected by sluggish streams. The wild uncultivated character of the downs has disappeared, and rolling hills have given place to tame rectangular fields and

trim hedgerows. The Easthampton property
lay about half-way between the downs and
the sea, and stretched away for some miles
along the banks of the muddy river Roding.
The park itself was on a gentle eminence, well
wooded without being picturesque, and commanding here and there pleasant peeps of the
sea on one hand and the line of downs on the
other. The house was a roomy, substantial
edifice of the Georgian period, boasting no
architectural beauties whatever, but solid and
comfortable throughout.

The shooting-parties at Easthampton were
not, as a rule, very lively affairs. In these
days, when field-sports are conducted on a
scale of luxury that would have made the
hair of our simple-minded forefathers stand
on end with amazement, not to say contempt,
it requires a variety of solid inducements to
prevail upon our "gilded youth" to honour
a country house with their sublime presence.
Not only must there be good shooting, but
the cuisine and the cellar must be of the first
order; and in addition to a lively party, including a fair proportion of frisky matrons,
fast unmarried girls, and "smart people"

generally, there must be an entire absence of restraint or discipline, and the motto of the house must be " fay ce que vondra." Smoking must be allowed the moment the ladies have left the dining-room, if indeed it has not already been initiated by some of the fair visitors themselves ; and a hostess who should even object to the smell of a cigarette in her bedrooms would probably be voted rather unreasonable. In short, the house must combine the selfish luxury of a club with the refinements of a private establishment, or the verdict will be "not good enough," and the gilded youth will betake themselves and their fascinations elsewhere. There are, it is true, a few old-fashioned houses still remaining— such, for instance, as we have endeavoured to depict in our representation of Sydmonton Place—where the well-known sporting character of the host, or the peculiar charms of the hostess, will continue to attract without the usual modern devices which have to be resorted to for the purpose of securing the modern guest. But such exceptional establishments are few and far between ; and the result is that the old-fashioned healthy tone of English

country-house life, which used to be at once
the admiration and the envy of foreign visitors
to this country, is gradually being supplanted
by an unwholesome reproduction of modern
fashionable life in London.

All this, however, has nothing to do with
Easthampton Park, the noble owner of which
would have been simply aghast if it had been
proposed to him to smoke in his dining-room,
and who had only lately, on the strong representations of his wife, consented to the appro-
priation of an exceedingly uncomfortable and
cheerless apartment in the vicinity of the
house-steward's room for the use of those who
could not exist without their tobacco. Easthampton was, in fact, a very quiet, and, it
must be confessed, a somewhat dull place
to stay at.   The shooting was of course only
moderate, according to modern ideas; gamb-
ling of any description, even down to penny
points at whist, was strictly tabooed; and
although no exception could be taken to the
eating and drinking, the society was of a
somewhat heavy order, and the evenings, despite Lady Narborough's praiseworthy efforts
to the contrary, were apt to be rather tedious.

But for those visitors whose principal objects were change, country air, and quiet, the place was not without its attractions. " Bear-fighting " is all very well in its way, and with a well-assorted party of congenial spirits may be carried on without any very serious results. But there are persons who cannot be got to see that there is anything amusing in having "hay" made in their bedroom during their absence, or being "drawn" by a lively party of ladies and gentlemen just as they are dropping off into their first sleep. It is needless to say that this form of diversion was unknown at Easthampton Park ; and although the propriety of "doing something to wake up old Narborough" had more than once been discussed by certain restless spirits who found themselves there for the first and only time, and one sprightly dame in particular had volunteered to lead a forlorn hope to the nocturnal storming of his private apartments, with the avowed object of assisting the noble earl into his bath at a time when such an immersion would probably have been extremely distasteful to him, these unhallowed designs never came to anything, and his lordship was

left in peace. On the whole, therefore, Easthampton Park had not a high general reputation in the fashionable world as a place
to stay at, and the occasional parties who
assembled there during the autumn and
winter months were certainly more respectable than lively.

To Gerard, however, who was scarcely in
a position to pick and choose to any great
extent, and who had not therefore been spoilt
by being made too much of, Easthampton was
a pleasant enough place to spend a few days
at. There was quite enough shooting to
satisfy his modest desires ; the Narboroughs
were always very kind to him, and made him
thoroughly at home; and having known Lord
Narborough all his life, more or less, he had
become used to his little peculiarities, and
less disposed to notice or be annoyed by them
than an ordinary casual visitor. Moreover,
at this time of year anything in the way of
a change from London was bound to be more
or less agreeable. So he had been looking
forward cheerfully to this visit, and arrived
at Easthampton, one fine October evening,
thoroughly prepared to enjoy himself, and for

the time, at least, to cast all thoughts of his other troubles behind him. From which we fear it will be argued that our hero was not so desperately in love as he would perhaps have wished it to be supposed.

CHAPTER XXXI.

IT was a lovely October afternoon. The sky was blue and cloudless; the woods had scarcely begun to put on their autumn colouring, and were dense and leafy as in June. Here and there a gleam of golden or russet foliage showed that some deciduous tree had succumbed to the mellowing influences of the advancing year; and on the uplands the cleared stubbles and an occasional plough already at work made it evident that harvest was over. But in other respects it might have been a golden afternoon in midsummer, and a glorious day for cricket.

A party of four guns from the Park had been engaged during the early part of the day in shooting partridges on the lower ground towards the river, and were now about to beat one or two small coverts on their way home. It was early for covert-shooting, particularly

in such an unusually fine autumn ; but some
pheasants were required for the house, and
the keeper was anxious to secure certain hares
whom he suspected of wandering proclivities,
before they should stray away from the covert
and fall a prey to his natural enemies, the
neighbouring small farmers.   As, moreover,
the gentlemen who were sent out shooting at
Easthampton were not invariably the most
deadly of shots, and were not unfrequently,
in fact, apt to be almost more dangerous to
their companions than to the game, he was
anxious to take advantage of having one or
two good guns out to make something of a
bag.   For on the present occasion the party
included not only our friend Gerard, whom
we have already seen to be a fair performer,
but an old General, a cousin of Lady Narborough's, who, when the walking was not
too difficult, was a very deadly marksman ;
and the Rev. Thomas Pilkington, the rector of
an adjoining parish, who was decidedly above
the average.   The fourth was an old college
friend of Lord Narborough's, a most estimable
character in every other relation of life, but
who, although manifesting a laudable anxiety

to distinguish himself with his gun, was perhaps hardly the sort of man whom an experienced sportsman would select as a companion in the field, and whose performances were regarded by the keeper with ill-disguised contempt.

It was now about half-past three, and the beaters were about to enter a thick belt of oak copse which skirted the north side of the park for about three hundred yards, and then, taking a turn to the right, ran out almost to a point along the banks of a little rivulet. A rough tangle of briars surrounded the whole, and within, a dense undergrowth of hazel and Spanish chestnut seemed to present an almost impenetrable mass of greenery, where pheasants might lurk with impunity, and laugh at the attempts of the beaters to get them up. These gentlemen now hung about outside, mopping their brows, picking nuts from the hazel boughs, and showing no particular inclination to plunge into the depths of the thicket before them. But Mr Underwood the keeper was inexorable, and proceeded to unfold his plan of operations.

"Now if you two gentlemen," he began,

touching his hat to the General and Gerard, " will go on pretty near to the end, we'll just bring it up to you, and the other two guns will keep ahead of the beaters, one on each side. There should be a few pheasants here, but it'll be terrible work to get 'em up, and they'll likely run on into the gyll yonder. We'll get some of 'em up at the end, though, and there'll very likely be some hares here too. You go along to the corner on the top side, Mr Courtenay, and you sir," addressing the General, " keep along the bottom ; you'll find it easier walking. Now men, set in ; we've no time to lose."

Away went Gerard along the top of the wood, until he arrived at the corner indicated to him, where he proceeded to take up a commanding position. The ground on this side of the wood was high, and commanded a pretty view across the park, with the calm sea shimmering in the distance on one side, and the hazy outline of the downs on the other. It was hotter than ever. Gerard had had a good deal of walking after the partridges, and felt rather lazy and sleepy. There was not a soul near him ; the wood was perfectly still; he could just hear the beaters beginning to struggle slowly along at the far end, but it would be a long time before they got near him, and he felt convinced in his own mind that no pheasant would be such a fool as to break from such a covert unless very hard pressed. And as for the hares, they might take their chance. So he established himself comfortably on a stile, with his gun across his knees, and began to think about Florence.

He had been staring vaguely before him for some minutes, in a comfortable state of drowsiness, and was very nearly falling asleep, when—whish—a splendid old cock pheasant skimmed out of the wood just over his head and shot away over the park. Tumbling off the stile, Gerard fired both barrels hurriedly after the bird, now a good distance off, but although he had evidently hit him, he had the mortification of seeing him continue his course with apparently undiminished strength, and make for the bottom of the park. "Hang it all! what a fool I was," he muttered, as he reloaded; "lovely shot that would have been, and I've tailored him too, I'm afraid," and relinquishing his seat on the stile, he was preparing to keep a better look-out when his ear caught a movement behind, and looking round he perceived that he was no longer alone.

The new-comer was a tall, powerful-looking man of apparently about sixty years of age. He might have been a good deal more or he might have been a good deal less; for although his hair was almost white, a short Vandyke beard and moustache were only here and there streaked with grey, and still for the most part a deep black. And although the weather-beaten and sun-browned face was seamed and wrinkled, the figure was erect and vigorous, and might have belonged to a man not very much over fifty. He was dressed in a slouched wide-awake hat and a dark suit of clothes of a somewhat nautical cut, and was smoking a very long cigar. He might, to all appearance, have been the captain of a foreign merchant vessel, or an American mining agent, or possibly an insurrectionist leader biding his time in England until a fresh opportunity for mischief should arise in his own country. He had, in fact, the general appearance of a foreigner in somewhat reduced circumstances ; but at the same time there was a certain look of dignity and breeding about him which convinced Gerard at a glance that the man was a gentleman.

"Ah," observed the stranger, taking his cigar from his lips, and speaking with the purest English accent, "you were just a little late for that cock, eh ? But you've hit him though," he continued, shading his eyes, and following the bird's course over the corner of the park. "Yes, he's down, and I think he's a dead bird too. You'll find him somewhere near the little bridge at the head of the pond by the forester's house."

"Who the devil are you ?" thought Gerard ; "you seem to know all about the place, anyhow. Yes," he replied, aloud, "I think he's down, but I bungled him frightfully. I ought to have killed him dead, but I wasn't looking out. They've only just begun to beat, and I didn't expect anything to get up so soon."

"Ah, just so," responded the stranger, showing by a nod that he appreciated the situation. "Rather early for covert-shooting, isn't it? You'll want some leaves off before you do anything much in that way."

"Yes," replied Gerard, "but they wanted some pheasants killed, so we're just having a turn through some of these small coverts outside."

"I see," said the stranger, looking about him with an appearance of interest. "I suppose you'll work along the gyll there afterwards, and finish up near the gate into the road?"

"Yes, I fancy that's what we're going to do," replied Gerard, keeping his eyes fixed on the wood, and determined not to miss another chance. "Wonder who the deuce he is," he thought to himself; "one of these queer friends of Narborough's, I suppose, who's just arrived. You know this place pretty well, I daresay?" he continued, without looking up, but feeling it incumbent upon himself to say something civil.

"Yes," returned the other, slowly, with a peculiar smile, which, if Gerard had seen it, could hardly have failed to attract his attention; "yes," he continued, "I have been here before."

There was something in the tone of his voice, as he said this, that caused Gerard to look up. But the peculiar expression had now passed away, and he was smoking imperturbably, absorbed apparently in his own reflections. And now a shot or two were heard from the other side of the wood, and the appearance of the Rev. Mr Pilkington round a corner about a hundred yards off showed that the beaters were beginning to draw near. A hare broke away in front of Gerard, and was promptly rolled over, and an old hen pheasant went back over the beaters' heads, successfully running the gauntlet of four barrels from the two guns on the flanks.

"Ah, there are the guns coming up," observed Gerard's friend; "I must be off now. Good-day! and don't forget that pheasant down by the pond." And getting over the stile upon which Gerard had been sitting, he disappeared in a moment.

"Who's your friend?" inquired Mr Pilkington, as he sauntered up a few minutes later, having first compared notes with Gerard as to what had been seen, killed, or missed during the beating of the wood.

"Haven't an idea," replied Gerard. "He's rather a rum 'un to look at; but he's a gentleman, I could see that plain enough. He must be some one who's arrived to-day, and come out for a walk alone. We shall meet him at dinner, possibly."

"Now then, gentlemen," said Mr Underwood, as he emerged with his red-hot beaters from the covert, "we'll just take the whole of the gyll there up before us. It's a good long beat, but there's sure to be some pheasants up at the end, and I've sent old Joe Diddums round to stop, so they won't run out. Two guns on each side, please, gentlemen; better not get too far forward at first, as they'll very likely come back. You come along of us this time, Mr Courtenay; you'll very likely get a rabbit or two, if you can see 'em."

The gentleman who rejoiced in the somewhat peculiar name of Diddums was one of those nondescript characters who are generally found hanging on in some undefined capacity to the out-door department of a large establishment. He was not exactly an under-

keeper, although he received pay as such, and
although no shooting-party at Easthampton
would have been considered complete without
his presence. He had been in his younger
days a notorious poacher, and more than
suspected of being in league with the gangs
of smugglers who at that time carried on
extensive operations along the greater part
of the southern coast. But as he grew older,
and as his old associates either disappeared or
paid the legal penalty of their delinquencies,
he became, if not a more respectable, at least
a less outwardly reprehensible character, and
had now for many years been attached to
Easthampton Park in the capacity of trapper,
ferreter, and general " odd man " in connection with the keeper's department. Nobody
knew exactly how old he was, but he had
been about the Park for the last thirty years,
and had been well known in the district for
some ten or fifteen years previously; so it
was generally assumed that he was between
sixty and seventy. But he was a wiry, hard-
bitten old man, who looked as if he had got a
good deal of vitality in him yet, and his
intimate acquaintance with every nook and

corner, not only of Easthampton woods, but
of the whole country for miles round, made
him, although a somewhat independent, yet
an exceedingly useful auxiliary to the head-
keeper at the Park.   He was a queer,
unaccountable old fellow, and would sometimes in the summer disappear for weeks and
months together, turning up, however, when
the shooting season began, just as if nothing
had happened, and always contriving to be
taken on the staff again.   He was anything
but a favourite with his lordship, who looked
upon him as a disreputable, not to say immoral
old man, and who had repeatedly threatened
to have nothing more to do with him.   But
his extensive local knowledge and varied
accomplishments had made him so useful to
the regular keepers that they seemed unable
to do without him ; and so, somehow or other,
year after year beheld Diddums just as much
to the front as ever.

So the party proceeded up Forman's Gyll,
as the long winding ravine was called ; and it
soon became evident that Mr Underwood was
right, and that there were some pheasants
here at any rate.   Three or four had already

got up in front, and fallen to the forward guns,
and one or two more had come back over the
beaters' heads. But just as they had got
about half way up the beat, where the wood
took a sharp turn round to the left, it became
evident to Gerard, who was outside, and who
from his position was able to command a view
of the far corner, up to which they were beating, that things were not going altogether
right in that direction.

"I say, Underwood," he called out to the
keeper inside, "there's something wrong up
at the end ; I can see the pheasants running
out like anything. There's half-a-dozen gone
right across the field already, and there's
another just going out now. I don't believe
there's any one stopping there, you know."

"What the deuce is the old fellow about ?"
growled the keeper, as he emerged from the
wood to survey the situation. "Darn the old
devil !" he exclaimed, "he's never got there
at all. Here, you beaters, stand steady a bit.
Bill," addressing an under-keeper, "you come
along o' me, and let's see what's up. You'd
better come too, Mr Courtenay, in case any
more get up. To think that old Joe should

play us such a trick, now. However, I'll be
even with the old 'un, see if I ain't."

A minute's run across the open brought
them to the far corner of the wood, one or two
more pheasants stealing out and fluttering
away as they approached. It was perfectly
clear that there was nothing to prevent them
from doing so, and it was impossible to say
how many might not have already escaped.

"Who'd have thought it now!" indignantly
exclaimed Mr Underwood; "there'd ha' been
just a nice lot of birds at this here corner,
and now just as likely as not they've all run
out. Howsomever, we must finish it out now.
You'd better stop where you are, Mr Courtenay. Come along, Bill; I'll give old Joe a
talking-to when I catches him, you see if I
don't."

He was just turning to rejoin his beaters,
when his eye caught sight of a figure sitting
crouched in a ditch about twenty yards from
the end of the wood. He stopped short, as
if shot. "Why, darn me if there ain't Joe
Diddums after all! Joe, you old devil, what
the blazes ha' ye been up to now?"

The delinquent Diddums was sitting low

down in the ditch, with his hands on his
knees, and staring straight before him.   The
healthy, bronzed hue that usually overspread
his weather-beaten features had departed, and
his face was ashy pale.   Large drops of
perspiration coursed down his forehead, which
he kept mopping in an aimless sort of way
with a red pocket-handkerchief, and his eyes
seemed starting out of his head.   He still,
however, retained his consciousness and voice,
occasionally ejaculating, "O Lord, O Lord!"
in a scared and horror-struck manner.   Altogether he presented the appearance of a man
who had received a sudden and violent shock
to his nervous system, which it would take
him some time to get over.

" Why, Joe, what on earth's the matter ? "
exclaimed Bill the under-keeper, less immediately concerned than his chief in the escape
of the pheasants.   " B'ain't you well, eh ? "

" Well ! " roared Mr Underwood, furiously ;
" he's drunk, that's what he is.   Get away
home, you old rascal, and I'll take care you
don't come out again along of us no more."

" No, he b'ain't drunk," said Bill, regarding
him attentively ; " leastways he har'nt had

northen' to drink since lunch-time, 'cos he's been alongside o' me the whole way. He looks regular skeart like ; seems to me more like some sort of a fit, maybe. Can't yer speak, Joe, and tell us what's the matter, man ? " shaking him gently by the shoulders. " Why, you look as if you'd seen a ghost."

" Ghost be hanged ! " growled Mr Underwood ; "it's drink, that's what it is. Why, he was well enough an hour ago. Shouldn't wonder if he's been and met some o' them poaching mates o' his, who've given him 'arf a bottle o' gin, likely. Why, Joe," he continued, though in a somewhat milder voice, " you've been and let away all them blessed pheasants, and spoilt the whole beat."

At these words the unfortunate Diddums appeared to be partially roused to a sense of his shortcomings. "Pheasants, ah, pheasants," he repeated, in a dazed sort of way, and stretching out his hand for his stick, which lay in the ditch beside him, he stood up, and began to tap against a tree in a vague sort of way, as if half conscious that this was what he ought to have been doing all the time.

" Ah, it's all very well to tap now," growled

Mr Underwood, " but they're all gone.   Well, if he ain't drunk, he's precious like it, that's all I can say.   Here, Bill, take the old beggar into the road, and send him home.   Best go with him a bit, and see if he gets better. You stop here, Mr Courtenay, and I'll go back and get this finished, though it's precious little use now."   And he hurried back to the beaters and the impatient guns in the rear, who were wondering what on earth was the cause of all this delay.

CHAPTER XXXII.

DIDDUMS.

"Sorry to hear there was a little *contretemps* about the shooting to-day, Gerard," observed Lady Narborough to our hero, who found himself sitting next to her at dinner that evening.

"Oh, well," replied Gerard, anxious to make the best of the affair, "it didn't much matter, you know. It was just at the end, and we had had a very nice day already; and after all, there the pheasants are, all the same, and there will be all the more to shoot next time."

"It was old Diddums' fault, wasn't it?" queried her ladyship. "I haven't heard all about it, but Narborough," glancing at her husband, "seemed very angry with him. I am afraid he must be rather a disreputable old man; but one doesn't quite like to send him away after being all his life about the place. Do you think yourself he was really drunk, or was he ill, or what was it?"

"Well, I'm sure I don't know," returned Gerard. "He didn't look to me the least as if he was drunk, and I don't exactly see how he could have managed it in so short a time. But then, again, he didn't look like a man in a fit, you know; no foaming at the mouth, or anything of that sort. No, what Bill the under-keeper said seemed nearest the mark, that he looked just like a man who had seen a ghost. The Gyll isn't haunted, by any chance, is it?"

"Not that I ever heard of," she replied, laughing, "and old Diddums doesn't look like a man who would be likely to see ghosts, does he? I'm sorry it has happened, though, for I am afraid Narborough is rather put out about it."

It certainly did appear as if his lordship was hardly in the best of tempers. He sat gloomily at his end of the table, evidently turning over the unhappy Diddums' long roll of delinquencies in his mind, and thinking how he could best get rid of him. He cared very little about the shooting; but that this wicked old man, with whose enormities he had put up for so many years, should have presumed to get drunk while on duty, as he felt convinced had been the case, and so bring discredit on his establishment, was not to be borne. He would dismiss him incontinently next day, and give orders that he should not be allowed about the place again. In the meantime he sat silent and grumpy, and made every one near him feel very uncomfortable.

"By the way," resumed Gerard, looking round the table, and anxious to change the conversation from the inconvenient topic of Diddums, "I expected to see a new arrival at dinner to-night. There was a man came and talked to me to-day, who seemed to take an interest in the shooting, and to know all about the place; and I thought he must be some one who had just arrived, you know, and came over for a walk."

"No, there's nobody come to-day," replied Lady Narborough. "Who could it be? What sort of a looking man was he, Gerard?"

"Well," returned Gerard, "he was rather a queer-looking fellow. Oldish man; tall, grey hair, short grizzly beard, and got up something like a sailor, I should say. But he talked quite like a gentleman, and seemed quite at home here. A pheasant of mine fell some way off, and he told me exactly where to look for it,—down by a bridge, he said, at the end of the pond near the forester's house."

"Bridge," grunted his lordship, who had been listening to the conversation from the other end of the table, "there's no b—b—bridge there; what on earth did he mean by talking about a b—b—bridge?"

"Well, to tell you the truth," said Gerard, "I didn't seem to remember any bridge there myself, and I've been down there several times. But he seemed to know all about it, and it wasn't worth while contradicting him."

"Oh, but you know, Narborough," chimed in Lady Julia, his lordship's maiden aunt, "there was a bridge there once, though it must be thirty or forty years ago, before you were born almost. I remember it quite well when we were children, your poor father, and your uncle, and all of us. We used to call it the Duck's Bridge, because the forester's ducks used to come and sit on it with their heads under their wings, and we used to drive them into the pond. It was a little wooden bridge, you know, and it gradually rotted away and fell into the water. Oh! it must be forty years since then, quite. Dear me! I wonder who your friend could have been, Gerard. It must have been some one who remembered the place in the old days."

But Lady Julia's reminiscences did not awaken any sentimental feeling in the heart of the present owner of Easthampton Park; on the contrary, the mere fact of an unknown stranger having presumed to display an acquaintance, and that apparently of long standing, with his ancestral domains, was enough to rouse his serious displeasure. "Some b—b—blackguard smuggling friend of Diddums', I'll be bound," he stammered out. "It was he who made him d—d—drunk, no doubt. What business has he hanging about here, I sh—sh—should like to know? I'll have the p—p—policeman up here to-morrow, and have him warned off the p—p—place, and D—D—Diddums too," he muttered, gradually working himself up into a passion, and getting red in the face with suppressed indignation.

" Well, I must say," put in Gerard, who, having introduced the topic of the mysterious stranger, and being, moreover, the only one of the party who had seen him, felt bound to stand up for him to a certain extent, " he didn't look the least like a blackguard ; and if he ever was a smuggler, he must have been a highly respectable one. He was dressed in a rough, outlandish sort of way, but I'm perfectly certain he was a gentleman, and I don't think you need be the least uneasy about him."

But Lord Narborough was not to be convinced. He had got into his head that the stranger was in some way or other connected with Diddums ; and when an idea had once taken root in his massive intellect, it required no ordinary agency to dislodge it. So he grunted, and choked, and muttered vengeance against Diddums and everything connected with him, and, in short, made himself generally unpleasant to every one at the dinner-table.

" Dear me !" resumed Lady Julia, in an undertone, towards the end of dinner, by which time the conversation had happily been diverted from the unlucky Diddums, "how strange it was that that man should have spoken about that old bridge! I haven't heard it spoken of for thirty years at least, and I had quite forgotten all about it. Oh dear! it makes one feel very old. Can't you remember what he was like, Gerard? I am trying to think of any one who it could possibly have been."

"Well, there was nothing very wonderful about him," replied Gerard. "He looked like a foreigner, and he looked something like a sailor too. But then he spoke English perfectly, and he had a way of speaking which sounded more like a soldier than a sailor. I mean, he spoke in rather a commanding sort of way, as if he was a bit of a swell when he was at home, you know. You see lots of men like him hanging about in London, but he wasn't the sort of man you'd expect to meet at the corner of a wood down here. But I think the less we say about him the better; don't you?" with a glance at his lordship. "I expect old Diddums will catch it to-morrow."

By the end of the evening, however, it

appeared that his lordship had to a certain extent recovered his temper. "I think it will be all right, Gerard," whispered Lady Narborough to our hero, as he lighted her candle for her. "Narborough has sent for Diddums to be here early to-morrow morning, before breakfast; but I think he only means to give him a good talking-to, and won't send him away this time."

But next morning, when Gerard came down to breakfast, being, as usual, rather late, things seemed worse than ever. Lady Narborough's face wore an anxious and troubled expression, as if she had been having "rather a time of it" with her lord, who sat sulkily at his end of the table, munching steadily at his breakfast, but scarcely deigning to address a remark to any one. A general feeling of discomfort and uneasiness appeared to pervade the whole party, and it was perfectly clear that something had gone very wrong.

"What on earth's up now?" thought Gerard, as he took a vacant place besides Lady Julia. "Diddums again, I suppose. What's the row?" he whispered to his neighbour; "his lordship looks as black as thunder."

" Oh, haven't you heard?" she replied, in the same tone. "Diddums never came this morning, and now it seems he has disappeared altogether, and Narborough's *so* angry about it."

"Oh, is that all?" returned Gerard. "Why, he's always disappearing and turning up again, isn't he? I thought he must have committed a murder at least."

"Oh, but it's such an odd thing for him to go away just now, you know, Gerard; and then Narborough thinks that strange man you saw has had something to do with it. He's really very angry."

"What rubbish!" muttered Gerard, who was perhaps less apt to be impressed by his lordship's little exhibitions of temper than his own immediate family circle. "They oughtn't to let him make such an ass of himself. So Diddums hasn't appeared, I hear?" he continued aloud, addressing himself cheerfully to Lady Narborough, but feeling much in the position of one who should attempt to make a joke at a funeral, or on any other equally inappropriate occasion.

Poor Lady Narborough did not answer,

except to look appealingly at Gerard. But his lordship had heard the observation, and took upon himself to reply.

"No, D—D—Diddums has not ap—p—peared," he stuttered out; "and what's more, I'll take good care he doesn't ap—p—pear at Easthampton again. I'll have no more of these s—s—sort of fellows about the place," he continued, gradually working himself up into a passion, and looking angrily at Gerard, as if he considered him in some way or other implicated in the affair.

"By Jove, what an odd thing!" remarked Gerard, unconcernedly. "However, it will save you any more trouble, won't it, his having gone away on his own hook?"

But his lordship did not appear disposed to see it in this light; and the General by no means mended matters by suggesting audibly to Lady Julia that there might possibly be a lady in the case; an insinuation which had the effect of producing something approaching to an explosion on the part of the noble host, and caused the immediate break-up of the breakfast party.

No further intelligence respecting the

absconding Diddums was received during
the day ; and, in fact, the remainder of
Gerard's visit passed away without anything
definite having been heard of him ; the result
being that Lord Narborough's temper, which
was apt to be affected by what to the world
in general might seem very trifling incidents,
became so exceedingly short that his guests
began to wish devoutly that Diddums and
everything connected with him were at the
bottom of the sea. " What the devil does he
want to make such a fuss about ? " growled
the General ; " the man's gone, and as he
never liked him, he ought to be devilish glad
to get rid of him. If I were my lady, I'd
be hanged if I'd stand such nonsense, or else
I'd give him something worth while losing his
temper about, hanged if I wouldn't, and see
how he liked that."

It certainly was rather curious that the old
gentleman should have suddenly disappeared
in this mysterious way, at a time of year, too,
when his services were in such requisition,
and when it was consequently to his own
advantage to be on the spot. And even if
it could have been proved that he had really

been drunk, it was hardly probable that the consciousness of his delinquency should have so weighed upon him as to make him consider it necessary to beat a retreat. He lived all alone in a little cottage on the Ashford Road, about a quarter of a mile beyond the little village of Easthampton; and a careful search over this secluded domicile revealed nothing that could throw any light upon his disappearance. His worldly goods and chattels were of a very humble and unpretentious order; but such as they were, they had been left undisturbed in their usual places. A theory that he had gone off on a poaching expedition was shaken by the fact of his rusty old single-barrelled gun being found hanging up on its usual hooks over the fireplace, together with the accompaniments of powder-flask and shot-belt. His rabbit-traps, too, were all lying together in a corner; and a closer search disclosed certain extremely suspicious-looking wires, which could hardly be said to form any part of the regulation equipment of an under-keeper. And, strangest of all, there was actually a small packet of tobacco, showing clearly either that he had left in such a hurry as to forget what to him was almost the staff of life, or else that he intended to return very shortly.

But no one had seen him depart; and nothing, in fact, was known of his movements after about five o'clock on the day of his disappearance, at which hour he had been left by Bill Simmons the under-keeper. This functionary had accompanied him as far as the village, and then, as he seemed to have to a great extent recovered, had left him to go home by himself. But Bill stuck to it persistently that he was not under the influence of liquor. "He went very queer as far as the village," he reported, "and kept muttering to himself as if he was dreaming; and then he seemed to get a bit better, and he says to me, says he, 'All right, Bill, I'll get home right enough now,' and then he looked me in the face just as if he wanted to say summat, but he didn't say northen', but he give me a squeeze of the hand, and off he goes as quiet as possible, though he still looked pretty bad. No, he worn't drunk, I'll take my oath, and he didn't smell o' liquor neither."

He had not gone off by train, for he was well

known to every one at the little station, and
nothing had been seen of him there.   But a
few days after his disappearance, the house-
steward, who had gone over to the market
town of Ashford, about twelve miles off, to pay
a visit to the landlord of the Bull Hotel and
posting-house, and who had of course imparted
the story to his friend, was informed, in the
course of conversation, that on the particular
day in question a carriage and pair had been
ordered to meet a gentleman at the station and
take him over to Easthampton, returning again
in the evening; that the carriage started with
the gentleman on the return journey about seven
o'clock, but that the driver was stopped all of
a sudden by the gentleman at a cross-roads,
about a mile from the village, to pick up a
man who appeared to be waiting there, and
who at once got into the carriage.   It was a
dark night, and the driver could not discern
the features of the man, who was, moreover,
muffled up in a heavy coat; but he was ordered
to drive straight to Ashford Station, where he
dropped both his passengers.   The gentleman
was described as a tall, elderly man, with a
greyish beard, and answered on the whole

to the description of the stranger seen by
Gerard. Doubtless, the driver of the carriage,
who had evidently been rather struck by what
had happened, might have had something
more to say on the subject; but unfortunately
he had left the hotel the very next day, having only been engaged on a temporary job;
and the landlord had not an idea where he
had gone to. Some importance, moreover, was
attached to the evidence of an under-gardener,
who had been at Ashford market that day,
and had gone to the station to see a friend off
by the nine o'clock train. A minute or two
before the train started, a fly from the Bull
had driven up, and two men had got out,
taken tickets, and got hurriedly into the train.
As they crossed the platform, the light from a
lamp fell on the face of one of them, who was
dressed in a slouched hat and a coat turned
up over his ears, "and for a moment," the
horticulturist averred, " I could have sworn it
were old Joe Diddums." But just as he was
about to step forward and address him, both
men got into a first-class carriage together;
" and then," as he sagely remarked, "of course

I knowed as it couldn't be Diddums, so I didn't
think northen' more about it."

By degrees, however, public interest in the
subject died out.   His lordship gradually recovered his temper, and in a fortnight's time
the disappearance of Joe Diddums had become
a matter of past history.

CHAPTER XXXIII.

RED TAPE.

THERE was confusion at the General Enquiry Office. From the Permanent Secretary down to the office-keeper's boy, an expression of concern, not to say dismay, sat upon every brow. Heads of departments went in and out of Mr Mill's room with grave and anxious faces, and junior clerks conversed together in groups in an undertone, exhibiting all the appearance of men who were weighted with a load of secret care and responsibility. Even the messengers went about with pursed-up lips and heads on one side, as if they were the depositories of secrets that, if revealed, might set the whole of Europe in a blaze, and shake the British Constitution to its foundation. In short, it was clear that something extraordinary had happened, and that a complication of an unusually serious nature had arisen in the internal organisation of this admirably conducted Government department.

To come shortly to the point, an appalling discovery had just been made, which threatened to seriously imperil the prestige and reputation of the office, to say nothing of ulterior consequences, the extent of which it would be absolutely impossible to predict. A document of indescribable importance was missing, and the united wisdom of the office was powerless to form the slightest idea as to what had become of it.

For some time past a commission had been sitting at Paris, composed of delegates from the International Office, the Aboriginal Office, and the French and Spanish Foreign Offices, to consider certain important questions in connection with the fisheries of the island of San Fernando, which, as every one knows, is one of our most thriving West Indian colonies, adjoining the continent of South America. The shores of the island had long been resorted to by French and Spanish, or rather Venezuelan fishermen, who claimed certain ancient fishery rights in those waters, but between whom and the islanders there existed a traditional feud, which on several occasions during the last two or three years had culminated in

serious disturbances, not always unattended
with bloodshed and loss of life. The matter
had, in fact, assumed such a serious aspect
that the constant presence of a British gun-
boat was considered necessary to preserve
order on the fishing-grounds, and despatches
and diplomatic notes innumerable had already
passed between the various governments concerned.

The Commission had now been sitting for
three or four months, and the commissioners,
finding doubtless that Paris was a very agreeable city in which to sojourn at the public
expense, showed no particular inclination to
bring their labours abruptly to a close. They
had, however, succeeded in delivering themselves of a preliminary report, and the matter
was to be brought before Parliament during
the approaching session, as a technical question had arisen respecting certain points in
the original charter of the colony of San
Fernando, upon which, in the opinion of the
law officers of the Crown, it was considered impossible to arrive at a decision without being
in the first instance formally submitted to
the Estates of the Realm. For this purpose

it was necessary to produce the charter, or
a properly authenticated copy. The charter
itself was in the keeping of the Governor and
Legislature of San Fernando ; but a copy of
it, together with other documents of equal
importance relating to the colonies, had
always been preserved in the Aboriginal Office
in London, until, in the course of years, they
had been handed over to the custody of the
General Enquiry Office. It was this document
that, on being required, was now found to have
disappeared.

It would be difficult to describe the con-
sternation that prevailed in the office when
this startling discovery became known. The
charters, letters patent, and other specially
important documents were all kept under
lock and key in the chief clerk's own room,
in iron-plated closets which were accessible to
no one but himself or some other person
deputed by him. The particular receptacle
wherein the copy of the charter of San Fernando
had been deposited had not been opened for
some time, and the pigeon-hole where the
precious document had reposed was found to
be coated with dust, showing that its dis-

appearance must have been of no very recent date. The chief clerk himself was of course above suspicion, and no amount of cross-examination could shake the asseverations of his assistants that they knew nothing about it. Such documents were very rarely required; and the last that could be remembered of it was that it had been had out about ten years previously, to show to some newly-appointed governor, when the chief clerk was able to swear that he had replaced it with his own hands. The wildest conjectures, as is usual in such cases, were freely hazarded on the subject. It was thought by some that, being on parchment, it might have furnished a meal for rats or mice, which were known to abound in the office; and the whole place was turned upside down to see whether the same fate had befallen any other document. Then it was suggested that the chief clerk, who was given to an occasional nap on quiet afternoons, might have walked in his sleep, and, jackdaw-like, have unconsciously secreted the precious document somewhere else. Suspicions, too, were directed towards the family of a char-woman employed at the office, whose eldest

son was known by the office-keeper to occupy
a prominent position in a Socialist debating
club in Bermondsey, and who might have been
a tool in the hands of political desperadoes.
But, anyhow, the precious charter was gone,
and no amount of speculation had the slightest
effect in casting a ray of light upon the cause
of its disappearance.

We regret to be compelled to state that the
member of the General Enquiry Office who
seemed least affected by this terrible national
disaster was the noble Vice-President himself,
who indeed exhibited an amount of equanimity
on the subject that to Mr Mills, the more experienced Permanent Secretary, was perfectly
incomprehensible.   He had been summoned
from Newmarket, much to his disgust, by
an urgent and somewhat obscurely-worded
telegram from his subordinate, and it must
be confessed that when the reason was explained to him, he by no means exhibited the
amount of interest that the occasion appeared
to demand.

"Well, my dear Mr Mills," he observed,
having listened with becoming gravity to that
official's tale of woe, "it's a great bore cer-

tainly; but, after all, it doesn't seem to me such a very awful thing, you know. I suppose we can't well get on without it, can we?"

"Good gracious, no, my lord!" replied Mr Mills, horrified at his chief's calmness; "it's certain to be called for the very first thing when the question comes on in Parliament, and it may very likely be wanted before that for the law officers. Why, I really couldn't say how soon it might be required; I should trust not within the next two months, but it's quite impossible to say."

"Well then, what's to be done?" inquired his lordship, standing in an easy attitude before the fire; "I suppose we must get hold of the original, and have another copy made. There is an original of the d——d thing somewhere, isn't there?"

"Good heavens! yes, my lord; the original is safe at San Fernando; that's to say"——
A fearful thought had struck him. What if it should all be part of some terrible Nihilist or Socialist conspiracy, and the original charter should also have been stolen by an agent sent out to San Fernando for the express purpose! Why, if the charter was gone, who was to say

that the island was really a British colony?
The question might be raised in the House of
Commons by some advanced Radical, anxious
for the dismemberment of the empire, and
how was it to be answered? In these revolu-
tionary days it was impossible to foresee what
Satanic schemes might not be hatching in the
brains of the leaders of some secret society,
and a plot might be on foot to undermine the
whole colonial empire by the simple process
of gradually abstracting the title-deeds of
each colony? And he, Mr Mills, the justly
esteemed Permanent Secretary, would be held
responsible for it all! The very thought
made him turn deadly pale, and he was
obliged to hold on to the back of an arm-chair
to support himself. "Oh yes, of course," he
continued, though in a somewhat faint and
hesitating voice, "the original is safe enough—
at San Fernando—of course. Oh no! nothing
can possibly have happened to that, I
trust."

"Well then, we'd better find out, hadn't
we?" observed Lord Ravendale, somewhat
astonished at the manner in which the Permanent Secretary appeared affected by what

had happened. "I'm afraid, you know," he went on, "I'm not so much concerned about it as I ought to be; but of course I'll do anything you think right. I suppose there's a telegraph to San Fernando, isn't there? We can just wire out and get an answer in an hour or two, I suppose, and then we can settle what to do next, eh?"

"Ah, my lord," almost groaned Mr Mills, "that's just the worst part of. It's most unfortunate, and seems a sort of fatality, but just at this moment we can't telegraph. I have inquired privately at the Aboriginal Office, and it seems that they are just changing their telegraphic cypher; the old one has been called in, and the new one won't be out at San Fernando for about three weeks yet; so they can only telegraph in clear—in the ordinary way, you know, and we couldn't possibly do that. It really is too unlucky, happening just at this moment of all others." And poor Mr Mills very nearly broke down.

"But why the devil can't we telegraph in the usual way?" inquired his lordship; "what harm can that do?"

"Oh, it would never do," replied Mr Mills,

shaking his head. "It would get about directly, through some clerk or employé, and the whole thing would be known everywhere. No ; the only thing will be to write a secret despatch, and we can't do that for another ten days now, till the next West Indian mail goes. Of course the Governor can telegraph back in clear, so that we shall understand, without making any reference to the charter; but we shall have to wait three weeks for that."

" Well then, we must just make the best of it," returned the Vice-President. " I haven't the slightest doubt myself that it's all right, you know. Why, who the devil would want to steal a d——d rubbishing thing like that? Of course I don't mean any disrespect to anything connected with the empire, and the Constitution, and all that sort of thing ; but between you and me, no man in his senses would want to steal a rotten old charter. Why, we shall probably find our own copy here before we get another from the colony. Oh no, it's all right enough, my dear Mr Mills ; I am sure you needn't make yourself uneasy."

But although the Vice-President's view of the case was decidedly encouraging, the Permanent Secretary was by no means altogether reassured. The official mind that has been nurtured for a long course of years on red tape and routine is not always amenable to the dictates of practical common-sense; and what might seem perfectly clear and intelligible to the ignorant and matter-of-fact outsider, will often present itself in a very different aspect to the highly-trained and timorous official.

"There is one thing we shall have to settle, my lord," he continued, "and that is, about getting the charter recopied."

"Well, that's simple enough, at any rate, surely?" returned his lordship; "why, some fellow out there can do it easy enough, can't he?"

"Oh yes, of course," replied Mr Mills, "but then, you see, it's not like copying any ordinary document. We shall have to get it sworn to very likely, and produce either the man who copied it, or else some one who can swear to having seen it compared with the original. We must be prepared for anything of this sort, you know."

"Well then, let them send the fellow over

who copies it, copy and all ; there's no difficulty about that, surely ? "

" Oh no, of course not, my lord. But, you see, this is rather a delicate matter, and one would prefer not bringing any ordinary clerk or copyist into it, if possible. It seems to me that, on the whole, the proper thing would be to send out some one from here who could bring the copy back with him, and if neces- sary, swear to having seen it compared with the original."

" Well, I must say that does seem rather a strong order," exclaimed his lordship, " to send a fellow the whole way out there and back on such a business. However, I'm all for doing the right thing, and if you think it really ought to be done, let's do it, by all means. But who is to go, eh ? "

" Well, the natural thing would of course be for the Aboriginal Office to send some one out, as it is, strictly speaking, a colonial matter. But if you don't mind, my lord, I should pre- fer, if possible, sending some one from here, so that we may keep the matter in our own hands, as it were ; and then, you know, we need really say nothing about it. The expense would come out of the Secret Service Fund, and we can keep it all perfectly quiet, I trust. Luckily, you have the power, as Vice-President of this office, of communicating direct with any ambassador, minister, governor,"— reading from a paper in his hand—"yes, 'Ambassador, minister, governor, or other representative of the Sovereign beyond seas, on any subject or matter connected with the archives of the said office,' so there will be no difficulty about it, and no one can ask any questions."

"Oh, I see!" laughed the Vice-President. "Yes, let's keep it dark, by all means; I'm sure I don't want to get the office into a mess. Well then, whom would you propose to send?"

"That's just it, my lord," replied Mr Mills, "It's rather difficult to think of any one. You see, it's leave time just now, and so many are away that it would be rather difficult to spare any one. Besides, too, although it would be a most important and confidential service, it's hardly one that we could expect any of the seniors to undertake, as it would simply be a voyage out there and back, with

perhaps a fortnight intervening ; and they are
mostly family men, and settled at home, and
might hardly care about that sort of thing.
It should be some young fellow who wouldn't
mind the knocking about, and whom we
could trust at the same time. I suppose
you couldn't spare Courtenay, my lord, for
a couple of months ? "

"H'm, well, I'm not sure about that,"
mused the Vice-President. "It would be
rather a bore being without a private secretary, certainly. Still, there's not much doing
just this moment, and I don't intend being
much in London 'till after Christmas, so I
might manage to get on without him. By
Jove," he thought to himself, "I've half a
mind to let him go. It would be a bit of a
run for him, and he seems rather down on
his luck somehow. Might do the chap good,
perhaps. Well, I'll think it over," he continued, aloud, "and I'll have a talk to Courtenay about it, and let you know to-morrow."

When the proposal was first made to Gerard
by his chief, who did not take long in making
up his mind on the subject, his first idea was
to decline. It was now about the middle of

November, and he had just completed his
arrangements for a little hunting. He did
not feel quite equal to making his first start
for the season in the Underdown country ;
but he and his two noble steeds had been
invited to Storrington for a fortnight, and
after that, he thought he might perhaps
summon up courage to go down to the en-
chanted region once more. The expedition to
San Fernando would of course take him at
least seven or eight weeks, and he could not
possibly hope to carry out any of his own
private operations till after the new year,
which seemed a great postponement and
delay. But on second thoughts he was
obliged to confess to himself that it was
not a chance that ought to be thrown away.
There was a certain amount of excitement,
too, about the whole affair, and besides giving
him a new experience and a glimpse of a new
country, an opportunity for which might not
occur again, it would be rather a feather in
his cap, and might possibly, in some way or
other, do him good as regarded Florence.
And finding that his chief, who really took
an interest in him, was all in favour of his

going, he soon made up his mind to accept the offer, and at once set to work to make arrangements for his departure. The horses were confided, not without a sigh, to the care of the trusty Martin, a hurried visit was paid to the paternal mansion in Somersetshire, and ten days later, Gerard, in company with a most imposing looking despatch-box emblazoned with the royal arms, was proceeding down the Southampton Water in the Royal Mail steamship "Iberia."

END OF VOL. II.

www.ingramcontent.com/pod-product-compliance
Lightning Source LLC
Chambersburg PA
CBHW031344070726
47496CB00017B/1713